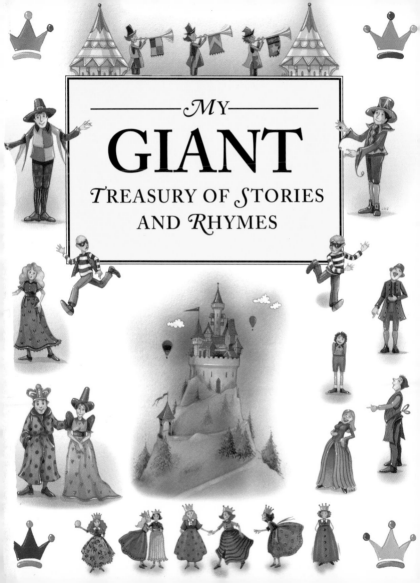

MY
GIANT
TREASURY OF STORIES
AND RHYMES

THIS EDITION PRODUCED FOR PROSPERO BOOKS
A DIVISION OF CHAPTERS INC

First published in 1999 by
Armadillo Books
An imprint of Bookmart Limited
Desford Road, Enderby
Leicester LE9 5AD
England

The stories and rhymes in this combined treasury
were previously published by Bookmart as
My Little Treasury of Stories and Rhymes in 1996
and *My Tiny Treasury of Stories and Rhymes* in 1998

ISBN 1-55267-038-4

Reprinted 2000

Printed in Singapore

CONTENTS

TEDDY BEAR TALES

FAIRY TALES

ANIMAL TALES

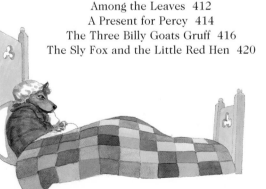

CHRISTMAS TREASURY

NURSERY RHYMES

POEMS FOR CHILDREN

TEDDY
BEAR
TALES

The Real Story of

THE TEDDY BEARS' PICNIC

Colonel Augustus Bearington (retired) here! The time has come to set the record straight about the illustrious event known as the Teddy Bears' Picnic. I was only a young bear at the time, but I remember it so well. Throw another log on the fire, Mungo. My threadbare old ears feel the cold.

First of all, you must remember
that things were different in those
days. Bears were less common then,
and only very lucky children lived with
a bear of their own. Today you young
bears live in homes that may have
four or five bears. You have company.

Children who shared their homes with bears usually spent most of their time in the nursery with a woman called a nanny. She looked after the children while their mother and father were busy—a job that any self-respecting bear could do in his sleep.

Children had to be seen and not heard in those days, and nannies got very cross indeed if they didn't wash behind their ears.

14

In those days, bears were not able to meet very often. The best chance was in the afternoon, when nannies took their charges to the park. Then children would play with friends from other big houses, nannies would chat and knit with other nannies, and bears, of course, could have a word with other bears. It was a part of the day that every bear looked forward to.

15

I think it was Rufus who first put the idea into our heads. Rufus was a reddish-brown bear from a rather well-to-do home. The little girl he lived with was a Lady. Yes, a real Lady, whose mother was a Duchess. But Rufus was a friendly bear, who never put on airs.

One day, Rufus told us that the Duchess was giving a special party for Very Important People. The Queen herself would be coming!

"You know, Gussie," said Rufus, "we bears should have a party of our own. We could invite all the Most Important Bears in town."

Well, the idea caught on at once. Every bear for miles around heard of the plan, and we soon had a guest list of over a hundred. But could we find a place big enough for the party?

Rufus didn't hesitate for a moment. "We'll hold it right here," he said.

It was obvious! I was a muttonhead not to have thought of it myself. After that, there was no time to lose. I was in charge, of course. It takes a military mind to organize an event on that scale. And I also came up with the date for the picnic.

Luckily, several young bears helped
with the preparations. You'd be amazed
what can be smuggled among a baby's
blankets. And we did not forget
cushions for the old bears.

At last the great day arrived. It
was the day of the Queen's Jubilee.
She had been on the throne for
umpteen years, and her subjects lined
the streets to cheer.

Meanwhile, dozens of bears padded along the back streets to the park.

What an afternoon that was! I met my dear Rosa—but that's another story.

What was that you said, Mungo? Yes, someone did see us. I don't know who it was. Yes, there was a song. It was quite popular, although the facts were quite wrong, of course. We were nowhere near the woods. All make believe? Just you look here. I've carried this worn photograph in my pocket for over sixty years.

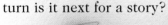

Stir the fire up, Mungo. The smoke's getting in my eyes. Whose turn is it next for a story?

The Amazing Story of

A BEAR WITH BELLS

Thank you, Colonel. I'm new to your circle, so let me introduce myself. I'm Hermann P. Bear from Switzerland. Now, with all respect, I've found that today's bears are just as brave and clever as the noble bears of yesterday. My story proves just that.

The story is about a friend of mine, back home among the mountains. I'll call him Fritz. He is a modest bear and, if he ever appears in public again, he would not want the world to know the part he played in the Great Zurich Bank Robbery.

Now Fritz is a jolly bear, but since the day he was sewn, he has suffered a great hardship. Around his neck, his toymaker put a collar of tiny bells. I can see you are horrified. Yes, poor Fritz could not move without jingling. He had to sit still, hour after hour, for fear of revealing our great secret.

Now Fritz was such an unusual bear that he was bought by a collector. Yes, a grown-up person who had over a hundred very beautiful bears. The grown-up was a rich man, who cared more about our value in money than the very fine bears we all were.

One day, this gentleman went to America to buy some more bears. While he was gone, he put all his dearest possessions in the bank, and that included some of us bears. We were kept in a trunk in a large safe-deposit box, where a bear only had to move a whisker to set off alarms and sirens.

25

We had been in the bank for two
long weeks, when the Great Robbery
took place. We heard an explosion
and felt ourselves being jiggled about
as the trunk was carried out, but we
couldn't see much through the keyhole.

It was some hours later, in a cold Swiss dawn, that the robbers arrived at their hideaway—a cave tucked away in the side of a mountain. They hid their truck and set about dividing up their ill-gotten gains.

All went well as they opened the boxes of gold coins and jewels, but when they saw us, they were very angry indeed. I'm afraid that the language of the unpleasant man who looked down at us was quite unrepeatable. My ears turned pink, I can tell you.

The stupid man had no idea we were valuable bears at all. He kicked the trunk so hard it toppled over, and we fell onto the cold floor of the cave, with icicles dripping down on us. My fur has never been the same since.

It was almost dark when we heard noises outside. It was the police! But the cave was well hidden.

All the robbers had to do was keep still. As you know, humans cannot hear bear speech, so we were powerless to make a noise, but Fritz was a very brave bear. He jumped to his feet and began to jingle and jangle as hard as he could. In the silence, it seemed to be an enormous noise. The most vicious-looking of the robbers leaped toward Fritz with a terrible cry. Just then, a powerful flashlight lit the dramatic scene.

Well, the rest is history. The robbers were caught, the loot was recovered, and we bears were taken into custody as evidence. Eventually, we were sold to new owners, all over the world.

And Fritz? Well, I cannot be sure. He fell behind a boulder and was not discovered with the rest of us. There are sometimes stories of a strange jingling sound to be heard in the mountains. I hope that Fritz is happy, living the life of a free and furry bear.

If you should ever find yourselves
in danger in the Alps, dear friends, I
like to think that a very old friend of
mine would come to your aid.

The Sad Story of
THE LITTLE LOST BEARS

The story of Fritz has made me think of an important subject. I am speaking, of course, of lost bears. I've never forgotten what my mother said to me: "Belinda Bear, always stay close to your owner, especially on trains, for there are many bears today sitting in Lost Property Offices."

Well, when I was a little bear, I did not always listen to my mother as well as I should. My friend Bessie and I got into all kinds of trouble. We spent more time in the bathtub than any bear would wish, having jelly, or paint, or honey washed out of our fur. But although we were often in disgrace, we were always careful not to get lost. The idea of the Lost Property Office was *too* horrible. We made sure that the little girl who looked after us *never* left us behind.

One day, Maisie (that was the little girl's name) went to visit her grandmother. And she went by train!

"Let's hold paws," said Bessie. "Then, if we get lost, we'll be together."

So Bessie and I went with Maisie on the train, and I can tell you that trains are *not* safe places for bears. First a lady squashed my ear with her shopping bag.

Then another lady with a little dog sat down nearby. The dog seized hold of Bessie's leg and tried to pull her under the seat!

Of course, we expect humans to be silly. They don't have a bear's sharp brain. But it was the train itself that caused our biggest problem. With every jiggle and jounce, it jolted us nearer to the edge of the seat.

It was sure to happen. As the train rumbled around a corner, we tumbled onto the floor and rolled under the table.

"We'll be left behind," I moaned. "It's the Lost Property Office for us."

But Bessie had one of her Good
Ideas. I listened carefully.

"If we climb inside Maisie's bag,"
she said, "we can't be left behind."

It *did* seem to be a good idea. We
climbed into the bag and fell fast
asleep at once.

It was dark when we
woke up. We could tell we
were no longer on the train.

"We must be in Maisie's
grandmother's house,"
Bessie whispered.

We soon heard footsteps.
The bag opened and a face
looked down at us. It was
the first lady from the train!

I don't know which of us was more surprised.

"Look!" she called to her husband. "These bears belonged to the little girl on the train. What can I do with them?"

It was then we heard the words we had been dreading.

"Take them to the Lost Property Office," said the man.

"We'll have to escape," said Bessie.

"Is that one of your Good Ideas?" I asked, but I knew that Bessie was right.

Late that night, we crawled out of a downstairs window and set off for home.

When morning came, we were deep
in a forest. Paw in paw, we wandered
through the trees.

39

Day after day, we walked on sore paws. We ate berries and slept among the mossy roots of the trees. Once a bad bird tried to peck out our fur to line its nest. Once I fell into a hole in a tree and only just managed to climb out. At night, we often cried ourselves to sleep.

One afternoon, we were found by a family taking a walk. The little girl brought me here to join you all and gave Bessie to her cousin. From that day to this, I have never seen Bessie or Maisie, and my furry face is often wet with tears. If there were human children listening to me now, I would tell them to cuddle their bears and keep them safe. I hope Maisie has found a new bear to make her happy.

The Scary Story of

THE GHOSTLY BEAR

Little bears, the story I am about to tell you is very, very scary. If you get frightened, you must put your paws over your ears and cuddle up to a grown-up bear. My aunty told me this story when I was a very little bear.

Once upon a time, in a faraway land, there was a huge castle. The castle stood empty for many years, but one day there was great excitement in the nearby village. The owner of the castle was coming to visit. Now no one had ever seen this mysterious owner, so there was a lot of talk about who it might be.

"I've heard it is a Countess," said the baker. "A witch put a curse on her. Now she wears a veil to hide her ugly face."

"No," replied the blacksmith, "the owner *is* a witch. She travels at night, and has a black cat."

"Nonsense!" The schoolteacher waved her stick. "It is simply an old lady who cannot move around very well."

Every day, the children in the
village looked out for the important
visitor, but no one came. Then, one
morning, a little girl called Lucy
noticed smoke rising above the
highest tower in the castle.

"She must have come in the night!"
she cried. "She must be a witch after all."

When they heard this, the villagers
were very worried. "We must take her
a big present," they said, "so she does
not get angry with us."

So a collection was made and a
beautiful chest was bought.

"Now," said the baker, "who will
give the present to the witch? I can't
go with my weak heart and
that path to climb."

"Nor can I," said the
teacher, "with my bad leg."

Only one voice spoke.

"I'll go," said Lucy.
"I'd like to see what she
looks like."

"But," said the blacksmith, "won't you be frightened?"

"Oh no," replied Lucy. "My teddy bear will keep me safe."

So Lucy set off to the castle. It was a long climb, but at last she stood before the great doors and knocked.

As she stood there, all by herself, Lucy began to feel just a little bit frightened. But she clutched her old bear and started to sing to keep her spirits up. With a horrible creaking noise, the doors of the castle slowly opened—all by themselves.

Lucy walked straight in.

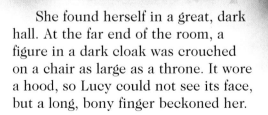

She found herself in a great, dark hall. At the far end of the room, a figure in a dark cloak was crouched on a chair as large as a throne. It wore a hood, so Lucy could not see its face, but a long, bony finger beckoned her.

When the little girl was standing in front of the figure at last, she tried to speak up bravely.

"Please, your highness, or your witchness, we wanted to welcome you to the castle and give you this present."

A horrible cackle came from the dark-robed figure. "A chest? I've got hundreds of them," it croaked. "But I can see that you do have something I want. Give me that teddy bear, and I will let you go home safely."

"No!" cried Lucy, hugging her teddy bear. "You can't have him."

"Really? Then I shall have to lock you up until you agree."

Lucy was dragged into a room with an enormous four-poster bed, and the door was locked behind her.

At dusk, the dark figure brought her some food and a single candle.

"Go to bed," it said.

 Lucy climbed into bed. She felt
very frightened, but somehow, she
managed to go to sleep.

At midnight, she was woken by a clock striking by her bed.

Dong! Dong!

She woke to find a large, white bear standing by her bed. He seemed to be shimmering with a strange light.

"W...w...what do you want?" she asked.

The strange bear said nothing, but it held out its paws toward Lucy's little bear, beside her in the bed.

"No!" cried Lucy. "He's mine!"

Then she saw an odd thing. The shining bear was crying!

He looked so very sad that Lucy could not bear it. "All right," she said quietly. "Here's my own special bear to cheer you up."

With a sigh, holding the little bear gently in his arms, the white bear melted through the door!

Lucy shut her eyes and rubbed them. When she opened them, she was back in her own room at home, tucked up in her own little bed. Only her teddy bear was missing.

Next morning, the whole village
gathered in amazement at the foot of
the hill. Overnight, the gloomy castle
had changed in an extraordinary way.
The windows sparkled. There were flags
flying from the turrets and doves
fluttering around the battlements.

"It must have
been bewitched
after all," gasped
the villagers. "Our
gift has broken
the spell."

Lucy thought about the chest
hidden under her bed.

"Someone was unhappy," she
thought. "And now they are not. That
is what bears are for."

I believe she was right, my friends. The mystery never was solved. It was said that the Countess who lived in the castle had suffered an unhappy childhood. Perhaps Lucy gave her back what she had lost.

The Funny Story of

THE BEAR WHO WAS BARE

My dears, after that scary tale, I have one that is not in the least bit frightening. Uncle Bill Bear here has a much sillier tale to tell you. It is about a bare bear—a bear wearing nothing at all, not even his fur!

Once there was a bear called
Edwin Dalrymple Devereux Yeldon III.
He said that his friends called him
Eddy, but as a matter of fact, this
bear did not have many friends. And
that was because he thought he was
better than other bears, with his long
name and fancy fur.

When the bears played leap-bear or hide-and-seek in the nursery, Eddy always refused to play. "Those are very rough games," he complained. "I might get my paws dirty. Games are too silly for superior bears like myself."

Well, after a while, all the other bears were sick of Edwin and his airs and graces. Some young bears tried to think of ways of teaching Eddy a lesson. But they did not need to. Edwin Dalrymple Devereux Yeldon III brought about his own downfall.

One day, Eddy was boasting about all the famous bears he knew. Some of the other bears wondered out loud if his tales were really true, which made Eddy furious. "You'll see," he said. "I'll write a letter to my friend Prince Bearovski. He's sure to write back at once, and then you'll see."

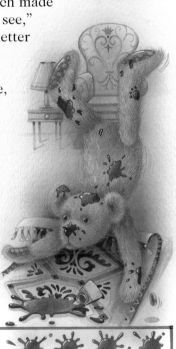

But as Eddy carried a huge bottle of ink across the room, his furry feet tripped on the edge of the rug. Down fell teddy Eddy. Up flew the bottle of ink. *Splat!* The bottle hit the floor, and ink flew everywhere! There was ink on Eddy's nose and ink on his ears and paws.

Teddy Eddy sulked for the rest of the day. But worse was to follow. Next morning, the little girl who lived there saw what had happened to her most beautiful bear. She decided that Eddy needed a bath.

The other bears peeked around the bathroom door to watch the proceedings. There were bubbles everywhere! Only the tip of teddy Eddy's nose could be seen. The watching bears giggled.

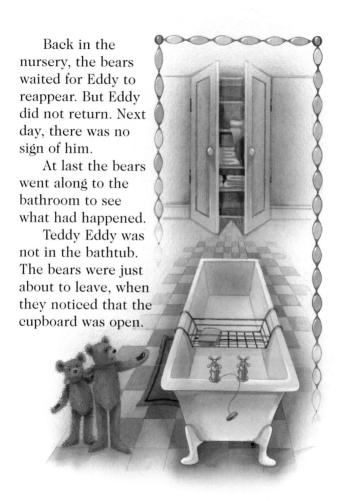

Back in the nursery, the bears waited for Eddy to reappear. But Eddy did not return. Next day, there was no sign of him.

At last the bears went along to the bathroom to see what had happened.

Teddy Eddy was not in the bathtub. The bears were just about to leave, when they noticed that the cupboard was open.

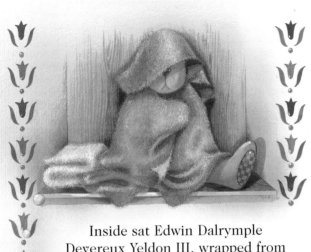

Inside sat Edwin Dalrymple Devereux Yeldon III, wrapped from ears to paws in a large towel.

"Come on, Eddy," called the other bears, "you must be dry by now, surely?"

"No," said Eddy. "I ... er ... can't."

"Oh come on," laughed the bears. And they tugged at the towel. Eddy tried to hold onto it, but it was no use. As the towel slipped away, every bear could see ... Edwin Dalrymple Devereux Yeldon III was bare!

When the little girl washed away the ink, Eddy's fur was washed away too. Poor Eddy. He couldn't hide any more. The old, proud Edwin Dalrymple Devereux Yeldon III was gone. A very different bear remained.

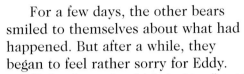

For a few days, the other bears
smiled to themselves about what had
happened. But after a while, they
began to feel rather sorry for Eddy.

"I think we should help him," said
one old bear. "He must be cold
without his fur."

"Why don't we make him some
clothes?" said another bear.

Over the next few days, the bears
had great fun. They used up all the
old scraps of material that they could
find and made some very grand clothes.

When he saw them, Eddy was overwhelmed by the bears' kindness.

"Thank you, my friends," he said, as he put on the clothes. "I will try to be a nice bear now. In following all that is good and kind and bearlike, I will be absolutely fearless. Or perhaps I should say, absolutely furless!"

The Short Story of

THE LITTLEST BEAR

Ha, ha! I enjoyed that story. But mine is stranger still, and much shorter. It is true that bears can change in many ways, but they cannot usually change their size. Anyway, my story is about a bear who was very, very small indeed. So small, in fact, that it was difficult to see him without a magnifying glass. One day, he came to this house—as we all did—and joined our little family.

What? No, there isn't any more to the story. I told you it was short. The bear was so small that he disappeared on the day he came here and has never been seen since. I imagine he is here with us now. Why don't you all take a look around?

The Unusual Story of

THE REAL TEDDY BEAR

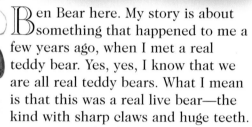

Ben Bear here. My story is about something that happened to me a few years ago, when I met a real teddy bear. Yes, yes, I know that we are all real teddy bears. What I mean is that this was a real live bear—the kind with sharp claws and huge teeth.

Here is what happened. My owner at the time was a little boy who was very fond of food. Wherever we went, he always made sure that he had a bag of goodies with him. Joseph (that was his name) felt happier if he had some provisions with him.

When he went camping with his friends, Joseph took extra supplies.

One year, we went deep into the woods. The boys put up their tents and went off to explore. Joseph left me in his tent. He looked at me very seriously and said, "Now Ben, your job is to stay here and guard the food!" And I was a young bear who took his job seriously in those days.

The boys were gone for a long time. I believe I dozed off for a while, because the next thing I knew, I was wide awake and listening to a very different sound. It was a snorting, sniffling, crunching, munching sort of a noise. I wasn't frightened, of course, but I did wish I knew just what was stomping and chomping outside Joseph's tent.

The sounds got louder and louder. Then I heard the sound of the tent flap being unzipped. *Zooooooooooop!*

A brown furry face peered in. It was a bear! A real bear!

For a long, long moment, I looked at the bear. And the bear looked at me. Then he opened his mouth and said, "Hello! Anything to eat in here?"

Well, you could have knocked me down with a feather. He was speaking bear language, of course, but I found it was not very different from teddy bear language.

Just in time, I remembered my duty.

"No," I said firmly. "No food in here at all."

But the bear was sniffing the air.
"Really?" he said. "I'm pretty sure
I can smell sausages and beans and
chocolate cake."

I thought quickly. "There *were*
sausages and beans and chocolate
cake, but the boys have eaten them."

"Any leftovers?" asked the bear. "Any crumbs at all?"

"None at all," I replied.

The bear nodded his head. "Ho hum," he said. "It's my birthday, you know. I just thought I might find a birthday treat around here. Well, nice meeting you." And as he ambled away into the forest, I'm sure I could hear his furry tummy rumbling.

Next morning, as planned, we packed up our things and set off for home.

"Now, have we got everything?" asked Joseph. "Let's go!"

By this stage, of course, I was well hidden in Joseph's backpack, so that the other boys would not see me. Otherwise I might have mentioned to him that the special emergency supplies bag had fallen behind the stump of a tree, helped along just a bit by a nudge from my elbow.

Joseph was a little upset when he found that his goodies were gone. But it was far too late to go back into the dark forest to find them.

As I sat on Joseph's pillow that night, I looked up at the big yellow moon peeking in at the window and imagined the friendly bear, sitting down in the moonlight to enjoy a special snack.

"Happy birthday, bear," I whispered. "Happy birthday!"

The Silly Story of

THE BUZZING BEAR

As most of you will know, I am Professor Septimus Bear. I have spent a good deal of my life looking into the different forms of bear talk, but one case made me appear to be a rather silly old bear.

I was living at that time in a large house. In the summer, children (and their bears) would come to visit my own family.

That was how I met the buzzing bear. He came to the house on a fine, sunny day. He was a large, fluffy bear, with golden yellow fur. Of course, I tried to make him welcome.

"Good morning," I said. "My name is Septimus. Will you tell me yours?"

"Buzz!" said the bear.

"Er … Buzz? Well, it's nice to meet you, Mr. Buzz. How was your journey?"

"Buzz!" said the bear.

"I'm sorry? Did you say that you have come from far away?"

"Buzz! Buzz! Buzz!" said the strange bear.

I was puzzled. I went straight to my books to find out if there was a country where bears only buzzed.

But all my research was in vain. There are hooting bears in Borneo and some singing bears in Thailand. But I could find nothing at all about buzzing bears.

At first I was disappointed. Then I realized the great opportunity that had been presented to me. I could be the very first bear to study this extraordinary language.

At once, I picked up a new notebook and pencil and set off to find the bear.

The buzzing bear was sitting rather sadly in a chair. I sat down beside him and began to take notes.

"Are you a bear?" I asked.

"Buzz!" he said.

Ah, I thought, one buzz means yes.

"Are you an elephant?" I asked.

"Buzz! BUZZ!" said the bear.

Two buzzes must mean no.

"Are you a giraffe?" I enquired.

"Buzz!"

My friends, I was very confused. Then I realized that the bear might not be able to understand me at all!

It was a beautiful day, so I took the bear by the arm and led him gently out into the garden. By the house was an enormous cedar tree. I led the bear up to it and patted its trunk firmly.

"Tree," I said. "Tree."

"Buzz!" said the bear.

I walked over to a shady seat.

"Chair," I repeated, pointing. "Chair. Chair."

You can probably guess what the bear said.

After half an hour, I had made no progress at all, and I was afraid that my reputation as a scholar was at stake.

At last, I invited the bear to sit down by a flower border.

We had only been sitting for a moment when, "Buzz! BUZZ!" Out of the strange bear's ears flew two big buzzing bees!

"What a relief!" said the bear. "I haven't been able to hear a thing with those bees buzzing in there!"

THE ADVENTUROUS BEAR

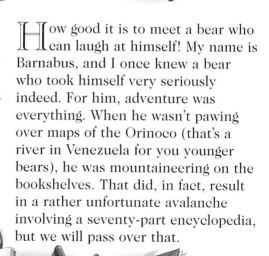

How good it is to meet a bear who can laugh at himself! My name is Barnabus, and I once knew a bear who took himself very seriously indeed. For him, adventure was everything. When he wasn't pawing over maps of the Orinoco (that's a river in Venezuela for you younger bears), he was mountaineering on the bookshelves. That did, in fact, result in a rather unfortunate avalanche involving a seventy-part encyclopedia, but we will pass over that.

Now, strangely enough, one of the volumes of the encyclopedia fell open at a page about a man who went around the world in eighty days. No sooner had he read this, than our friend—let's call him B.—decided he would be the very first bear to travel right around the world.

"You will need to beware of sharks," said an old seafaring bear.

"You will have to look out for icebergs," said another. "The white bears who live on them are very fierce."

"Don't forget to send us some postcards," said a little bear.

B. spent months preparing for his trip. By the time he was ready, he had so much equipment, he could hardly walk.

"Good luck!" everyone called, as he staggered off.

Well, eighty days passed. And then another eighty. There was no news from the adventurer.

Then, one morning, a postcard arrived. It showed a picture of the Eiffel Tower. On the back, there were just three words: *Reached France. B.*

The following month, a postcard showed the Leaning Tower of Pisa. The message said: *Crossing Italy. B.*

A few weeks later, a card showed the Great Wall of China, with the message: *Learning Chinese. B.*

Next month, the excited bears waited for a postcard to drop onto the doormat. At last it came, showing a Spanish flamenco dancer. The message read: *In Spain. B.*

The older bears looked puzzled and shook their furry heads. Sure enough, when they looked closely at the postcards, everyone could see that all of them had been sent from a town just a few miles away.

"I think some of us need to go on an expedition too," said the older bears.

This time, the bear expedition returned before nightfall, bringing with them a very crestfallen young bear.

"I did try," he said, "but the world is *so* big!"

The oldest bear put a fatherly arm around my shoulders. "We are just happy to have you home," he said. "Come in and tell us all about your adventures."

Oh, I see that I have given the secret away!

Yes, my friends, I was that foolish young bear. And I can tell you I am happier to be here with you than in Turkey or Tasmania or Thailand!

The Christmas Story of

BEARS EVERYWHERE

Mungo here! My story reminds us of a time of year that is very special for bears. Yes, I mean Christmas. Many bears move to new homes then, as they are given as presents. But we bears have a special job to do at Christmas.

Now, you know that humans make the kind of mistakes that sensible bears would never make. At Christmas time they are worse than ever. Sooner or later, some silly human is likely to send the wrong present to the wrong person.

We bears, who understand how important it is to feel loved and wanted, know that someone who receives the wrong present will feel upset. So that is why our special job at Christmas is to look out for misplaced presents and send them back to where they belong.

One Christmas, a forgetful granny in England made a particularly bad mistake. She sent woolly gloves to her niece in Australia, where it is hot at Christmas time, and a sunhat to her niece in Canada, where the snow lay thick on the ground. And to make matters worse, she sent them at the very last minute.

What could we bears do with so little time to spare? Even last-minute flights from both countries would not arrive in time. A council meeting of the Growling was called at once, and the Oldest Bear of All was consulted.

"Dear bears," he said, in his quavering voice, "I can see only one solution, and it is one that we can use only in the most serious cases. These presents will have to be … *ahem* … lost … until Christmas is over. Please alert the bears concerned at once."

Just as soon as messages could reach the bears at opposite sides of the world, action was taken.

The parcel with the gloves was dropped carefully behind a cushion. The package containing the sunhat was tucked into a cupboard.

Now normally in this kind of situation, action is taken immediately after Christmas. The presents are exchanged and then allowed to be discovered. But for some reason, both sets of bears in this case forgot all about the "missing" presents.

In fact, it was not until six months later that teddy bears in Australia discovered the offending package. In horror, they at once contacted their Canadian cousins, and that parcel was retrieved as well. Now both sets of bears were at a loss to know what to do.

The bears reported to the next meeting of the Growling. There were gasps of horror around the room. Then the Oldest Bear of All told those bears what he thought of them.

"Sir," said one of the guilty bears, "we will make the exchange at once."

But at this the Oldest Bear smiled. "I think you will find," he said, "that no exchange will now be necessary. Simply allow the presents to be found. But make sure that this NEVER happens again."

The bears did as they were told. The niece in Australia was delighted with her gloves. The niece in Canada just loved her sunhat. Which of you clever bears can tell me why the presents did not need to be changed?

The Secret Story of

THE BEARS WHO WERE BRAVE

fter that *seasonal* story, Mungo, it is my turn. My name is Bella Bear, and my story tells of two bears who both did a very brave thing.

The first bear was called Walter. He was a very fine bear in every way, but he was very afraid of dogs. When he was young, a poodle chewed one of his ears and he never got over it.

The second bear was Hannah. She simply could not stand heights.

Both Hannah and Walter lived with a little boy called Joshua. But when Joshua's baby sister was born, Joshua said he was too old for teddy bears, and he gave them to the baby.

In fact, Joshua was a little bit upset by the amount of attention that the baby received, so his parents gave him a baby of his own—a little puppy called Jack. Jack went everywhere with Joshua, and he really was rather like a baby. He whimpered when he was hungry, and he made little puddles!

One day, Walter and Hannah were left in the garden at lunchtime.

Suddenly, the bears heard a frightened little bark. Somehow, the naughty puppy had managed to climb onto the roof of the summerhouse. He was stuck.

"We must rescue that puppy," said Hannah.

"Hmph," said Walter.

"Joshua loves him," Hannah reminded him.

"All right," said Walter, "but you can do it, because I'm not going anywhere near him."

"But I can't go up there!" cried Hannah. "It's much too high!"

The two little bears sat miserably together. Then both spoke at once.

"I'll go if you will," they said.

So Hannah and Walter helped each other up onto the summerhouse roof and showed the silly puppy how to get down.

None of the humans in the house know how brave the little bears were. But the puppy knew, and I think he told Joshua, because a few days later, the little boy decided that his sister was too *small* for bears, and he tucked Hannah and Walter into *his* bed again.

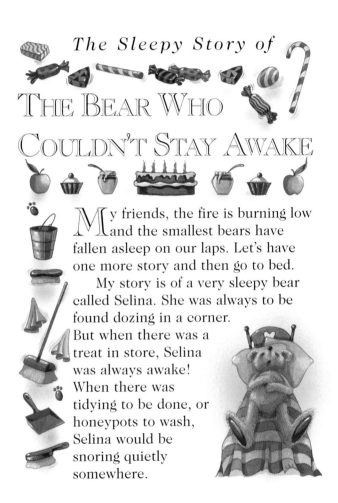

The Sleepy Story of

THE BEAR WHO
COULDN'T STAY AWAKE

My friends, the fire is burning low and the smallest bears have fallen asleep on our laps. Let's have one more story and then go to bed.

My story is of a very sleepy bear called Selina. She was always to be found dozing in a corner. But when there was a treat in store, Selina was always awake! When there was tidying to be done, or honeypots to wash, Selina would be snoring quietly somewhere.

98

"If you ask me," grumbled the Oldest Bear of All, "that lazy little bear is just pretending. She needs to be taught a lesson."

"Bears do need their sleep," explained her friend Marilyn. "And Selina has slept right through suppertime. She wouldn't do that if she was really awake. She's always very hungry."

The older bears shook their heads. "If she is pretending," they said, "she will wake up after we are asleep and have a little snack then. We must stay awake tonight and watch."

As it grew dark, five bears took up their positions and watched the sleeping Selina.

Very soon, the first little bear's bright eyes began to close. In just two minutes, he was fast asleep.

The second little bear struggled hard to stay awake, but soon he too was dreaming a teddy-bear dream.

The third bear was older than the first two. He was quite determined to stay awake. He decided to march up and down—quietly, of course. *Pad, pad, pad,* he marched across the floor. *Pad, pad, pad,* back he came. *Pad, pad, pad … pad, pad, pad.* He looked as if he was awake. He sounded as if he was awake. But that bear was sleep-walking!

The fourth and fifth watching bears decided to keep each other awake. They talked in whispers late into the night. But soon the whispers became gentle snores.

In the morning, the other bears crowded round.

"Well ... *ahem*," said the first bear, "I certainly didn't see her wake up."

"Er ... neither did I," agreed the second bear.

"I was on duty all night," said the third bear, "and I didn't hear a sound."

"I saw nothing unusual," said the fourth bear, truthfully.

"Nor did I," replied his friend.

So the mystery of the sleeping bear never was solved. But Selina gave an extra loud snore and the tiniest, sleepy, secret smile.

Now it is time for little bears everywhere to go to sleep. Goodnight, little bears! Goodnight!

Ten Little Teddy Bears

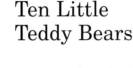

Bears often decide to have picnics, and just as often, things don't go exactly according to plan. Once ten little bears planned a picnic.

One little bear tried to catch a butterfly and didn't come back for hours. Another attempted a somersault, and couldn't get up again.

The third bear went swimming, when he should have been helping. The fourth got the hiccups and was no use at all.

The sixth little bear was stung on the nose by a bee,

because he wondered if
its honey might be tasty.
The seventh got so
excited that she had to
have a rest! Her
sister was chased by
a crab. She forgot all
about making sandwiches.

It was not surprising
that the ninth little teddy
bear decided to go home.
So the tenth bear tucked
into the buns and cakes all
on his own, and was soon a
very full little bear indeed!

At last, all the little
bears did gather together
for their party, but after all
the excitement, they fell
fast asleep ... every one
of them!

Goldilocks and the Three Bears

Once upon a time
there was a very
naughty little girl
called Goldilocks. One
day she went for a
walk in the woods and found a little
cottage. The front door was
open, and Goldilocks went in!

In the kitchen, the little
girl saw three bowls of
porridge. Feeling hungry,
she took a spoonful of the
porridge in the biggest bowl.

"Ugh!" she said. "That
is far too hot!"

She tried the next bowl.
"Ugh! That is too cold!"

Finally Goldilocks tried
the smallest bowl. She

didn't say a word – she was too busy eating! The porridge was just right.

When she had finished, Goldilocks looked for somewhere to sit down. In the living room were three chairs. She tried the big one first, but it was far too hard. The she tried the middle-sized chair. But she didn't like that one either. At last Goldilocks sat in the little chair. It felt just right, but ... crash! ... Goldilocks was *too* heavy!

"I need a rest," said Goldilocks,
going upstairs to the bedroom.
She climbed onto the largest bed, but
it was too hard to sleep on.
Next she tried the middle-sized bed,
but that was too soft. So Goldilocks
tried the smallest bed. It was perfect!
Goldilocks fell fast asleep.

Just then, the three bears who
lived in the cottage came back from
their walk. At once they saw that
something was wrong.

"Who's been eating *my* porridge?"
asked Father Bear in a growly voice.

"Who's been eating *my* porridge?"
asked Mother Bear in a soft voice.

"And who's eaten *my* porridge –
all of it?" squealed Baby Bear.

In the living room, it was the same story. *Someone* had been sitting on each of the three chairs.

"Follow me," said Father Bear sternly, and he tiptoed up the stairs. "Someone's been lying on *my* bed!" he exclaimed.

"And someone's been lying on *my* bed," said Mother Bear.

"And someone's been sleeping in *my* bed," squeaked Baby Bear, "and she's still there! Look!"

At that moment Goldilocks woke up to see three angry, furry faces. She jumped up and ran straight home. And she never was *quite* so naughty again.

109

The Teddy Bear Who Had No Clothes

Little Katya had a very special birthday present.

"I'll call you Teddy Thomson," she told her new bear.

Next morning, when Katya went to school, she had to leave Thomson behind. He looked forward to meeting the other toys. But as soon as Katya had gone, he heard them giggling.

"I can hardly look. It's so *embarrassing*!" said the rag doll.

"It shouldn't be allowed!" giggled the baby doll.

"At least I have paint!" puffed the big blue train, blowing his whistle.

"I feel sorry for him really," said the clown.

Teddy Thomson couldn't think what they were talking about.

"My dear, surely you *know*!" gasped the rag doll. "You haven't any clothes on!"

"You're a *bare* bear!" chortled the train. "We can't play with you if you don't wear *something*."

Suddenly Teddy Thomson felt really silly. "What are teddy bears like me *supposed* to wear?" he asked.

The rag doll hunted in the toy box. "Here's my best dress," she said. "The one I wear for parties. You can wear it instead."

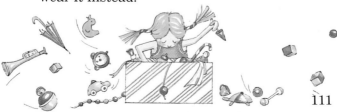

So Thomson put on the dress, which really fit him quite well. Then he looked in the mirror.

"Nothing in the world will make me wear this," he said firmly.

"I've got a spare suit," said the clown, helpfully. "And a slightly squashed spare red nose."

So Teddy Thomson put on the suit and the nose and went to the mirror again. "This is even *worse*," he cried.

"I've got something that suits everyone!" giggled the baby doll, handing Teddy Thomson a square of white material.

"Never!' growled Thomson.

"Then there's only one thing left," chugged the train. "We must paint you!"

Half an hour later, when Katya came home from school and saw Teddy Thomson, she burst into tears. "What's happened to your beautiful fur?" she cried.

So Katya bathed her teddy bear and took him outside to dry. And Teddy Thomson, deciding that he didn't *need* clothes or paint to cover his beautiful fur, sang a little song:

> "A bear isn't bare
> If he's wearing his fur.
> He's not at his best
> In a clown suit or dress.
> Being covered in paint,
> I'm bound to declare it,
> Was simply not *me*.
> I just couldn't BEAR it!"

113

The Big Bad Bear

"You can play wherever you like in the woods," said Mrs. Bear to her twins, "but what ever you do, don't disturb the Big Bad Bear!"

"What is a Big Bad Bear like?" whispered Buttons to his sister.

"He's big and … he's bad … and he's … a kind of bear," said Lily. "And I think I see him! Run!"

But when they had finished running, she thought that perhaps she had only seen a bear-shaped bush after all.

"What do Big Bad Bears eat?" asked Lily.

"Oh … berries … and nuts … and insects … and … little bears," said Buttons. "And I think I can hear him coming! Run!"

But when they had finished running, he thought that perhaps he had only heard the wind after all.

"What does a Big Bad Bear look like?" asked Buttons, nervously.

"He is very tall … and he has very big teeth … and he has very long claws," said Lily. "And I think I see him behind that tree! Run!"

115

But when they had finished
running, she thought that perhaps it
was only a bird in a tree after all.

Lily listened and noticed that the
birds weren't singing. The leaves
weren't rustling. There were no
scampering, scuttling noises at all.

"It's *too* quiet," she said. "And I
think I can see someone coming! Run!"

The two little bears ran until
they were gasping for breath and
could hardly see where they were
going. Then ... crash! ... they fell
over something lying under a tree.

Lily screamed,
"Aaagh!"

Buttons yelled,
"Aaagh!"

116

And the Big Bad Bear saw them both and shouted, "Aaagh!"

Then they all looked surprised.

"You're not very big and you don't look very bad," said Lily to the Big Bad Bear.

"I'm *not*!" said the little bear. "That's just my name."

"That's silly!" said Lily. "Names and bears should be alike."

The Big Bad Bear laughed. "You're right," he said. "Let's play. But first, what are *your* names?"

Tall Tree Trouble

There is one very important thing to remember if you are going to climb a tree – you have to be able to get down again. It's a pity that Teddy Bellingham didn't think of that before he set out one morning to climb the tallest tree in the garden.

It was harder than he had thought it would be. For one thing, the branches didn't seem to be in quite the right places. "This is a badly designed tree, from a climbing point of view," said the bear to himself, as he struggled to reach the next branch. After a few more branches, he was very tired indeed.

Teddy B. decided that it was time to have an official rest. In fact, he'd had a few *unofficial* rests already. He sat on a branch and swung his legs and looked down at the garden. It was a mistake. When the little bear looked down, he really couldn't help noticing what a *very* long way from the ground he was.

But Teddy B. was a brave little bear, so on he went, paw over paw toward the top.

It wasn't until his next official rest that Teddy Bellingham noticed that the tree was *moving*.

"Ooooh," moaned Teddy Bellingham, "I'm beginning to feel just a little bit queasy."

It was time for even a very brave bear to head for home. Poor Teddy Bellingham managed a few branches but then he had to admit, he was well and truly *stuck*. He sat on his branch for a long time. A cold, worried feeling grew in his tummy.

"No one knows I'm here," he thought. "I could stay here for ever!"

Suddenly Teddy B. noticed that the branch he was sitting on grew straight toward the house.

Very, very carefully, he crawled along the branch. At last he could reach out his paw and *just* touch the window. It was shut.

Teddy Bellingham groaned. But adventurous bears don't give up just like that. He broke off a twig and used it to tap on the window.

Through the glass he heard the little boy he lived with say, "Listen to that tree tapping. It's spooky!"

"It's not spooky, it's *me*!" thought Teddy B. And to show that he wasn't a tree, he began to tap out a pattern. Da da da, da-da-da. In no time at all the little boy had opened the window and rescued his bear.

"Of course, I *could* go back and finish climbing that tree today," said Teddy B. to himself next day. "But it might be boring if I do it *too* often...."

The Little Lost Bear

Once upon a time there was a teddy bear who kept getting lost. He fell behind the shelf in the toy shop and by the time he was found, Christmas was over and all the other bears had gone to good homes.

But one day, a man came in who was on a business trip. He wanted to take a present home for his little girl.

"This little bear is just what I need!" cried the man. "Elise has been wanting a bear like this for ages."

He tucked the little teddy bear into his coat pocket and got back into his taxi. But the man arrived late at the airport and had to run to catch his plane. As he ran, the little bear fell out of his pocket.

It was not until the evening that the bear was found again.

"Just look!" said a smiling woman in blue overalls. "This teddy bear will be perfect for my little nephew." She put him in one of the pockets of her overalls. But that night, she threw her overalls into the washing machine without thinking.

Swoosh woosh! Soon the little bear was cleaner than he had ever been in his life! In the morning, the smiling woman's husband went outside to hang out the washing. No sooner had he put down the laundry basket, than a naughty puppy came along and carried the little bear off in his mouth. Puppies love to bury things, but the puppy's owner saw him starting to dig and cried out, "No, Bouncer!"

The puppy dropped the little bear and ran to his owner. A minute later, a seagull swooped down and picked the bear up in its beak.

124

This seagull soon got tired of carrying the little bear. It flew over the sea and dropped the little bear onto the deck of a cargo ship below.

"Well," said the captain. "I'll keep this little bear in my cabin."

When the ship at last arrived at port, the captain went to visit his sister in a nearby town, taking the bear with him. As he walked down the path, his niece ran to meet him.

"Uncle George!" she cried. "Have *you* brought me a present? Daddy forgot last time *he* went away."

The captain held out the little bear.

"Here you are, Elise," he laughed.

There's a Bear in the Bathroom!

"Hey!" yelled Charlie one evening. "There's a bear in the bathroom!"

"Charlie!" shouted his mother. "I've got enough to do looking after the baby, without listening to silly stories from you."

The bear smiled at Charlie.

Charlie looked
carefully at the
very large bear.
"*What*," he said,
"are you doing in
our bathroom?"

"It's a very
nice bathroom,"
said the bear in a
low and growly
voice.

"But how did
you get here?"
asked Charlie.
The bear didn't answer but it looked
a little guiltily toward the window,
and Charlie could see some pretty
large paw prints on the window sill.

"You can't stay here," he said to
the bear. "You'd better come into my
room."

127

"That's awfully kind of you," said the bear. "I don't suppose you have any … er … little snacks?"

Charlie took the bear to his room and gave him a half-eaten bag of soggy potato chips.

"Were you planning to stay long?" he asked, politely.

"If you like," replied the bear with a smile. "I thought perhaps you might like some company at the moment."

Charlie sighed.

It was true. Ever since his little baby brother had been born a few weeks before, it seemed that no one had any time for *him*. Charlie didn't like the baby. All day long it dribbled or cried. If *he'd* done that, he'd have been sent up to bed.

"I'm very glad you've come," said Charlie to the bear. "But you're going to have to be careful not to be found."

"I'll blend into the background," said the bear.

Charlie was doubtful, but in fact the bear turned out to be rather good at hiding himself.

129

Before long, Charlie and the bear became very good friends. Everyone else could make a fuss of the baby: Charlie had a special pal. When he was sad, the bear gave him a big furry hug. When he was happy, it made funny bear-faces that made Charlie laugh so much his tummy ached.

One day, Charlie went downstairs to find some apples for the bear and got a surprise. In the living room, his little brother was standing up!

He looked up, smiling all over his little face, and said, "Charlie!"

"Yes," said his Mum. "That's your big clever brother."

Charlie sat down and played with his brother. He was even warmer and cuddlier than the bear.

That night, when Charlie went to bed, he thought of telling the bear all about his baby brother. But he wasn't very surprised to find that the bear was nowhere to be seen, and there were big black paw prints on the window sill.

The Horrible Hat

"Please," begged
Little Bear, "don't
wear that hat."
It was Parents' Day at
Little Bear's school, and
his mother was getting
ready to set off.
"Don't be silly, Little Bear," she
said, picking up the big purple and
orange hat. "It's a beautiful hat."
Little Bear hid his face in his
paws. His mother did her best to
embarrass him on every occasion.
Probably nobody else's mother would
be wearing a hat *at all*.

Little Bear followed his mother miserably to the car. Dangling feathers tickled his nose all the way to the school.

When Mrs. Bear got out of the car at the school, everybody turned to look at her. Little Bear wished he was even smaller. He wanted to curl up and never see any of his friends again. But his mother was striding toward the school, calling and waving.

Little Bear did the only thing he could. He hurried off to hide in the coat room.

In another room, Old Boffin Bear was showing an experiment to some parents when something went horribly wrong. There was a burst of orange flame and the next minute little flames were dancing along the desk.

"Fire!" yelled Old Boffin Bear. "Everybody out! Follow me!"

Outside everybody was present and correct ... except one.

"Where's Little Bear?" cried Little Bear's mother. "I'm going back in!"

The rooms were filled with smoke, but she found a little gap of clear air near the floor. So she crawled on her paws and knees.

Little Bear crouched in the cloakroom. Then he thought he saw something moving through the smoke. It was round and orange and it had purple dangly bits all round. Little Bear had never been so pleased to see that hat!

When Little Bear and his mother appeared in the playground, everyone clapped and cheered.

"Oh dear," said Little Bear's teacher. "Look at your beautiful hat, Mrs Bear." It was true. The hat was blackened by smoke and the edges were drooping.

"Don't worry," said Little Bear, giving her a big hug. "I'm going to save up and buy you an even *bigger* hat. Just you wait and see."

The Most Beautiful Bear

"I am the most beautiful teddy bear in the world," thought Mopsybell. Her fur was fluffy. Her paws were pink . Her eyes were bright and shiny. She was sure that the next little girl to come into the shop would want her.

"She'll love me and look after me and keep me safe and warm," thought Mopsybell. "And I'll live in the kind of house that is just right for a beautiful bear like me."

Just then a little girl *did* come into the shop with her grandmother.

"Now Juliette," said Grandma. "You may choose any teddy bear."

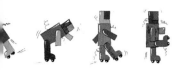

The little girl scowled.

"I don't like bears," she said. "They're for babies. I'd much rather have a robot."

"Don't be silly, dear," said Grandma. "What about that big beautiful bear in the window?"

Mopsybell wriggled on her shelf. She was going to be chosen! But the little girl groaned.

"That's the most stupid-looking bear I've ever seen," she said.

Mopsybell was so shocked, she nearly fell off the shelf. What a *horrible* child!

Juliette was looking at a model dinosaur with huge teeth. "I'd rather have this," she said. "It reminds me of *you*, Grandma."

But Grandma was firm. "I know you'll love this bear, dear," she said.

"I am still the most beautiful bear," thought Mopsybell as they went home. "Juliette will know that as soon as she has a good look at me."

Sure enough, when Grandma had taken Juliette home and hurried off to catch her train, the little girl took a long hard look at her bear.

"I *can* think of some uses for you," she said.

All too soon, Mopsybell found out what she had meant. Mopsybell was just the right size for Juliette's parachute experiments. Tied to a pillow case, she was dropped out of all the upstairs windows.

Then Juliette decided to grow things instead. She tied Mopsybell to a stake as a bear scarecrow, to keep birds away from her seeds!

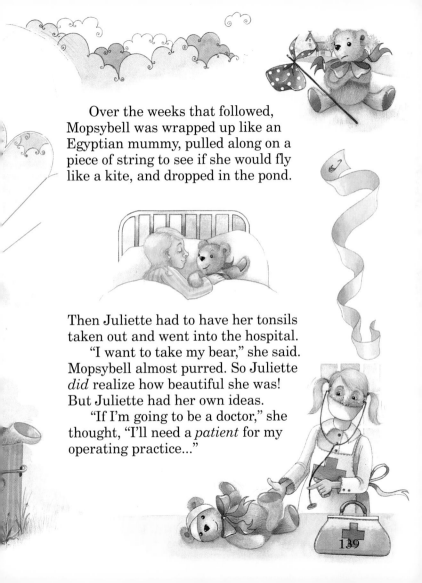

Over the weeks that followed, Mopsybell was wrapped up like an Egyptian mummy, pulled along on a piece of string to see if she would fly like a kite, and dropped in the pond.

Then Juliette had to have her tonsils taken out and went into the hospital.

"I want to take my bear," she said. Mopsybell almost purred. So Juliette *did* realize how beautiful she was! But Juliette had her own ideas.

"If I'm going to be a doctor," she thought, "I'll need a *patient* for my operating practice..."

139

Mr. Bear's New House

Da, da, dum, dum. "I've never heard such a dreadful noise," groaned Mr. Bear. His neighbour was playing his drums again. "There's only one answer," thought Mr. Bear. "I'm going to have to move."

The next morning, Mr. Bear set out to find another house. The first one he looked at seemed perfect. Mr. Bear was about to say, "I'll take it!" when the house began a strange sort of shivering and shaking.

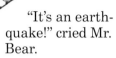

"It's an earth-quake!" cried Mr. Bear.

"Did I mention that the train station is very convenient?" asked the agent who was showing Mr. Bear round.

"*Too* convenient," said Mr. Bear.

The next house seemed much better. There were no trains for miles around. Mr. Bear opened his mouth to say that he would like to move in, but his words were drowned out by a screaming, roaring, rushing overhead.

"Sorry," said the agent, "I didn't hear you. Planes do low-flying exercises over this hill."

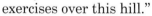

141

"This is no good for me," said Mr. Bear firmly. "Isn't there anywhere that is far away from trains or planes or any kind of noise?"

"It's funny you should say that," said the agent. "I've got just the place."

Half an hour later, Mr. Bear was in a boat being rowed toward a lighthouse. Mr. Bear explored it.

"I like it very much," he said. "But what is that noise?"

"What noise?" asked the agent.

"*That* noise," said Mr. Bear. "A coming-and-going wooshing noise."

"I can't hear anything," said the agent. "Except the sea, of course."

"Ah," said Mr. Bear. He thanked the agent and went home. When the drumming nextdoor began again, Mr. Bear just smiled. "I do believe he's improving," he said.

143

The Exciting Life of Uncle Bobo

"So you want to be a pilot, my lad?" said Uncle Bobo to his nephew, Henry Bear. "Ah, I remember my first days flying an S29... I'll never forget looping the loop over your grandma's house one day. I was so low that some of her laundry got caught on the tail and I flew back to base with grandpa's underpants flying out behind!"

"Gosh," said Henry. Maybe he wouldn't be a pilot. It would be better to do something that no one in the family had ever done before.

"I've decided to be chef," he said.

"Ah, a chef?" said Uncle Bobo, when next he visited. "Did I tell you about the time I was chef to Prince Bruinski? I remember when the King of Oursania fell into one of my giant cakes. It took them three days to find him. How we all laughed!"

"Goodness," said Henry. Perhaps he wouldn't be a chef after all. That day he saw an interesting word in the dictionary. "I'm going to be an ent-o-mol-o-gist," he told his family. "It's someone who studies insects."

145

A few days later there was a postcard from Uncle Bobo. On the front was a picture of a tropical forest. Henry read the card with a sinking feeling in his tummy. "Dear Henry," it said. "Greetings from my entomological tour of Brazil. This morning I discovered three species of giant ant previously unknown to bear. Best wishes, Uncle Bobo."

Henry sighed. There must be *something* that Uncle Bobo wasn't an expert at. He thought long and hard. By the time Uncle Bobo came to his birthday party, he had decided.

"When I grow up," he said, "I'll be the most famous Henry in the world."

But Uncle Bobo didn't hesitate.

"Goodness me," he said. "It seems only yesterday that I changed my name from Henry to Bobo."

Henry almost cried.

"Don't tease Henry, Bobo," said Aunt Hilda. "You've only had one job in your life. Tell him what you do."

"Can't you guess?" asked Uncle Bobo. "I make up stories for children. And they could be about anything you can think of ... even myself!"

Henry felt better. "When *I* grow up," he said. "I'm going to be a writer. And I'll have lots to say about *uncles*."

Bears Everywhere

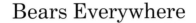

Joseph was the easiest boy in the world to please. He liked *anything* with bears on it. He had bears on his slippers and bears on his socks. His bedroom curtains had bear paw prints all over them. He had lots of stories about bears, and on his bed sat his own special teddy bear, Rufus.

Joe loved Rufus best of all. He told the old bear all his secrets and all his worries. And Rufus seemed to understand.

One day Joe's cousin asked him to visit.

"You can help Joe to pack, Katy," Joe's mother told his big sister. "You *would* have been invited too, if you hadn't put gravy in Aunt Sue's purse." Katy grumbled all the time as she helped to pack Joe's clothes.

"Joe, what are you *doing*?" she asked.

"I'm putting Rufus in," said Joe. "He doesn't really like being inside, but he might get lost on the train."

"But you can't take *Rufus*!" laughed Katy. "Everyone will think you're a real baby. Baby Joe, Baby Joe, has to take his teddy bear!"

Joe put Rufus back on the bed. He felt a cold space in his tummy.

Later on, in the train with Aunt Susan, he almost forgot about Rufus. And it was exciting seeing the farm and the animals.

But Joe was very quiet as they had supper. Later, he lay very still in the strange bedroom opposite his cousin's. There were roses on the wallpaper. In the dark, they looked like ogres' faces.

"Oh Rufus," said Joe, "I wish you were here."

During the day, Joe almost forgot that he was sad. But at night he couldn't sleep. Aunt Susan was worried.

"He won't tell *me* what's the matter," she said to her husband.

"Why don't you try?"

Uncle Richard sat on Joe's bed.

"You know," he said. "When I used to stay with my Granny, I never felt homesick because I took my old bear, Mr. Bumble, with me. He was my best friend." Then Joe told Uncle Richard all about Rufus and how he missed him. Uncle Richard smiled.

"I guess I could get along without Mr. Bumble for a night or two, if you'd like to borrow him."

Joe opened his eyes wide.

"But you're older than *me!*" he said.

"Just a bit," grinned his uncle. "What has someone been saying to you? Just between you and me, Joe, I feel rather sorry for people who don't understand about teddy bears, don't you?"

Grandfather Bear Goes Fishing

"I'll be back this evening, dear," said Grandfather Bear to Grandmother Bear. "I'm going to have a nice quiet day fishing down on the river."

"Why you want to go sitting around on drafty riverbanks, I'll never know," grumbled his wife.

"I'll wear my warmest coat, dear," murmured Grandfather Bear, as he left. He was looking forward to a long, peaceful day, sitting on the riverbank.

Grandfather Bear soon found a good place to sit, where passing bears would not disturb him with chatter.

"Peace and quiet at last," said Grandfather Bear. But five minutes later, someone coughed behind him.

"It's only me," said little Bruno Bear, who lived down the road. "Mrs. Bear was worried your ears would get cold. So I've brought your hat." Grandfather Bear couldn't be angry.

"Thank you very much," he said.

Just as Grandfather Bear got settled, he was disturbed again. It was his friend from next door.

"Your wife asked me to bring your scarf," explained the friend. "It *is* rather chilly today."

"Thank you," said Grandfather Bear a little irritably.

Grandfather Bear took a deep breath of country air. All at once, a horrible noise shattered the peace of the riverbank. It was Grandfather Bear's nephew on his motorbike.

"What are you doing?" cried the old bear in dismay.

"Sorry," said his nephew. "But Aunty was sure you would need a hot snack. I brought it as fast as I could so that it wouldn't get cold."

Grandfather Bear sighed. Come to think of it, he did feel a little bit empty somewhere behind his third waistcoat button.

When he had eaten his snack, Grandfather Bear felt full and warm and happy. He settled down for a little snooze after his snack.

Seconds later he heard a voice.

"Mr. Bear! Are you all right?" It was Maisie from the Post Office.

"Mrs. Bear knows that I always take a walk along the river at lunchtime," she said. "She asked me to bring you this flask of coffee."

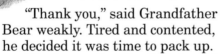

"Thank you," said Grandfather Bear weakly. Tired and contented, he decided it was time to pack up.

"I'm home, dear," called the old bear, as he walked into the hallway. Grandmother Bear hurried to meet him. "Did you catch anything?"

Grandfather Bear raised his eyes to the ceiling. "No dear," he smiled. "Not even a cold!"

155

Harold Hubertus Bear

Harold Hubertus Bear, HH to his friends, was no ordinary bear. His great grandmother had been a Princess among the royal Russian bears. His mother came from a long line of bears who had rubbed paws with Dukes and Countesses. In fact, he was a very well connected bear indeed.

HH was a kind bear and many people were very fond of him, but he was rather pompous and liked to hear the sound of his own voice. In fact very little happened in Bearport that Harold Hubertus didn't express an opinion about.

"When it comes to matters of importance," he would say. "You need a bear who has seen a bit of life."

"It's high time that bear came back down to earth," said Mr. Bloomer the baker. "Any ideas, Basil?" Basil, his nephew, looked thoughtful.

157

A few weeks later the whole town was buzzing with news. Princess Ursula Berelli was coming to visit Harold Hubertus.

"She's a rather distant … er … cousin, I think," said Hubertus.

Harold Hubertus worked hard to make sure that the visit would be a success. He had several rooms in the Hall redecorated. He had six extra gardeners working on the lawns and ten extra cooks in the kitchen.

By the time the great day arrived, HH was exhausted. At the agreed time, a very small car swept through the gates and up to the front door. Harold Hubertus was amazed. Out stepped the Princess. She wore a little crown on her head and more jewelry than HH thought was quite right in the daytime. Nevertheless, he greeted her with a deep bow.

"Dear Princess," murmured HH, "has your car broken down?"

The Princess laughed aloud.

"Nobody who is *anybody* drives a large car nowadays, Humphry."

The Princess allowed herself to
be led into the dining room, where
the tables were piled high.

"Dear Horribilus, I'm afraid I
never touch anything richer than a
slice of toast. Why not give this food
to the people of the town?"

"What a charming idea," said HH
with a gulp. "I'll tell the servants to
take it away at once."

"Tell me, Hardboiledus," cried the
Princess, "are you really so behind
the times as to have servants? I can
hardly believe it."

"Er … that sort of thing is no longer done, I suppose, in your circle?" enquired HH in a shaky voice.

"Goodness me no, Hurglegurglus," laughed the Princess. "I will help you to take all this delicious food to the good townspeople!"

It was not until he was waving her goodbye, that HH noticed that the Princess was wearing a bracelet that read, quite clearly, *Basil*.

"I fear," he said to himself, "that I have been a very foolish old bear. But everyone else is happy and that makes me happy too. And only a bear with real pedigree can take a joke as well as I can, after all."

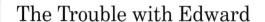

The Trouble with Edward

"Where's that bear?" roared Mr. Teddington from the garage. "Someone – and I think I know who – has filled my boots with mud!"

Edward tried to explain.

"I was trying to start a wormery, dad. We've been learning about worms at school."

"Come here at once and clean out these boots!" replied his father.

It didn't seem to matter what he did, Edward was always in trouble. Even if he was trying to do something helpful, it always seemed to go wrong.

Later that day, when she had finished cleaning up after Edward, Mrs. Teddington flopped into a chair.

"What *are* we going to do with that bear?"

"I think the problem is that he doesn't have an older bear to look up to and copy. I thought we could invite your friend Violet and her boy Billy to stay with us," said her husband.

"*Two* boys in the house?" Mrs. Teddington shuddered. But she remembered Billy handing out hymn books very quietly at her sister's wedding and reluctantly agreed.

As soon as Billy arrived in the house, Mr. and Mrs. Teddington felt that they had done the right thing. Billy was clean and polite, but more important, he was *thoughtful*.

163

Billy polished Mr. Teddington's car so that you could see your face in it. *And* he saved the rinsing water for Mrs. Teddington's potted plants.

"He's having a very good effect on Edward," whispered Mrs. Teddington to her husband. "Although sometimes I think he is just a little bit *too* good."

On Billy's last day, the whole family went for a picnic by the river.

"We're a little too near the river for safety," said Billy. "One false step could cause a dangerous situation."

"Oh nonsense," cried Mr. T. "It's perfectly safe." But as he spoke, he slipped. SPLASH!

"He can't swim!" yelled Mrs. Teddington. "Somebody do *something*!"

"Dad!" cried Edward. "I'll save you!" and he plunged into the water.

"I shall stay safely away from the edge," said Billy calmly. "People are often drowned trying to save someone."

But Mr. Teddington climbed out of the river with a broad smile.

"In case you hadn't noticed, Billy," he said, "the water only came up to my knees. I *know* accidents can happen even in shallow water, but Edward is a very good swimmer and there are things that are more important than being sensible. I'm very proud of Edward."

Mrs. T. gave them both a big hug. "There wasn't any need to worry," smiled Mr. Teddington.

"I wasn't really worried," said his wife. "Especially now I can see *exactly* where Edward gets his ... Edwardness from!"

A Bear at Bedtime

O ne bear in a bed is cuddly,
and two are better still.
With three teddy bears, you
are sure to be warm, and just
one more is no problem at all.

Five teddy bears in a bed can
help you sleep, while six teddy
bears are very good indeed. Seven
is a lucky number for bears. And
eight teddy bears are best of all.

But nine teddy bears in a bed?
Be careful! There may not be room
for you...

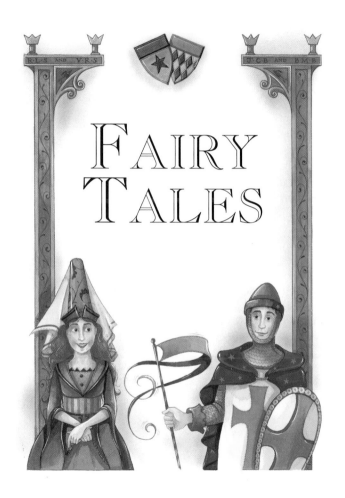

FAIRY TALES

HANSEL AND GRETEL

There was once a woodcutter whose beloved wife died, leaving him to bring up two young children. After a while, the woodcutter married again, but soon times became hard.

The new wife soon became tired and sad. One day she said to her husband, "We do not have enough food for all of us. Let's take the children into the forest and leave them there. Perhaps someone else will find and feed them."

Meanwhile, the woodcutter's children had been listening..

"Don't worry, Gretel," said the little boy, whose name was Hansel.

The next day, the family went deep into the forest. As they walked, Hansel dropped crumbs from a crust, hoping to follow them back home again. But the birds soon ate the crumbs, and when the children were left all alone in the forest, they were completely lost.

Hungry and afraid, Hansel and Gretel wandered through the trees. Suddenly, they saw a cottage made of candy and gingerbread!

But no sooner had the children munched into the house, than a sharp voice shouted, "Eat your fill, dear children!"

It was a witch! She bundled the children into her house.

The witch made Gretel work for her, while she kept Hansel in a cage. Every day, she asked him to poke his finger out of the cage to see if he was fat enough to eat!

At last the day came when the witch could wait no longer. "Stoke up the fire," she said to Gretel, "and put your head in the oven to see if it is hot enough."

But Gretel said, "You'd better check yourself."

When the witch poked her head into the oven, Gretel gave her a huge push and slammed the door shut.

Quick as a flash, Gretel set her brother free. Gathering up the witch's treasure, the children ran from the house. A little bird showed them the way home. Their stepmother had gone back to her own people, but their father was overjoyed to see them.

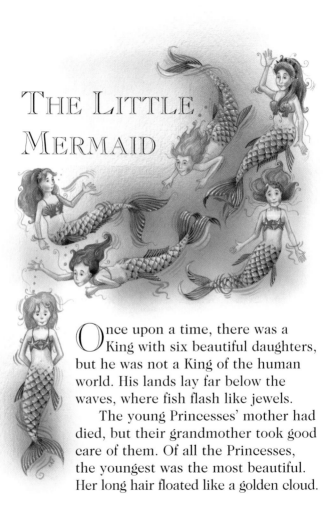

THE LITTLE MERMAID

$\bigcirc$nce upon a time, there was a
King with six beautiful daughters,
but he was not a King of the human
world. His lands lay far below the
waves, where fish flash like jewels.

The young Princesses' mother had
died, but their grandmother took good
care of them. Of all the Princesses,
the youngest was the most beautiful.
Her long hair floated like a golden cloud.

The girls loved to hear their grandmother tell them stories of the land above the waves. There, she told them, human beings walked on strange things called legs.

The youngest mermaid longed to see it.

"When you are fifteen," her grandmother said, "you shall go."

When the eldest Princess was old enough, she swam to the surface, returning the next day to tell of the wonderful things she had seen.

Year after year, one after another, the mermaid Princesses grew old enough to swim up to the world of humans. At last, the time came for the youngest mermaid to see the world she had longed to visit.

As she rose to the surface for the first time, the sun was just setting. Nearby, a fine ship was sailing. As the little mermaid watched, a handsome Prince came onto the deck. He did not know that he was being watched, or that the little mermaid could not take her eyes from his face.

Darkness fell, and the ship began to toss as the wind rose. A dreadful storm wrenched away the sails and the rigging, and huge waves crashed onto the deck. As the ship sank, the little mermaid saw the Prince, struggling in the water. She held up his head and guided him gently to shore. When morning came, the wind dropped and the sun rose. The little mermaid stayed near the shore to watch over the sleeping Prince.

Before long, some girls came along. The Prince woke as they bent over him on the sand. Only the little mermaid felt sad.

After that, the little mermaid often rose to the surface, eager for a sight of the Prince. At last, she could not bear it any more. She decided to go to see the powerful Water Witch.

The Water Witch laughed when she saw the little mermaid. "I know why you have come," she said. "You want to go and live in the human world, so that you can be near the Prince. But do you know the price you will have to pay?"

"No," whispered the Princess, "but I will pay it gladly to be human."

"I shall need your voice, with which you sing so sweetly," said the witch. "Then I can turn you into a lovely human girl. But remember, if the Prince does not love you with all his heart and take you for his wife, you will turn into sea foam and be lost forever."

"Hurry," said the mermaid. "I have already decided."

So the Water Witch gave the little mermaid a potion to drink.

As soon as the little mermaid stood for the first time before the Prince she loved, he wanted to meet her and, although she could not speak to him, he soon found that he could not bear to be apart from her.

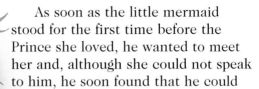

The little mermaid loved the young man more each day, but he never thought of marrying her.

Months passed, and the Prince's mother and father urged him to find a bride. At last he agreed to meet a Princess in a nearby country. Of course, the little mermaid went with him, but she felt as if her heart were breaking.

When the Prince stepped on shore
and met the new Princess for the first
time, he was so dazzled by her beauty
that he decided to marry her at once.

The wedding was a magnificent
affair, with flowers and silks and
jewels. Everyone cheered
with joy to see the
happy pair. Only
the little mermaid
was silent. Her
tears fell
unseen.

That night, the little mermaid stood on deck and gazed at the dark water. At dawn, she would be turned into foam.

But as she stood there, her sisters rose to the surface of the water. Their flowing hair was cut short.

"We gave it to the Water Witch," they said, "in return for this knife. If you kill the Prince tonight, you will be free of the spell."

The little mermaid took the knife, but, as dawn broke, she knew that she could never harm the Prince.

Weeping, the little mermaid plunged into the sea, but instead of turning into foam, she found herself floating in the air. Around her were lovely creatures made of golden light.

"We are the daughters of the air," they said. "You can be happy at last with us."

As the little mermaid rose into the sunshine, she looked down at the Prince's ship and she smiled.

SLEEPING BEAUTY

Once there lived a King and Queen who were overjoyed when a baby girl was born to them.

It seemed as though everyone in the kingdom was invited to a grand feast for her. The most important guests were the twelve fairies who make special wishes for children.

At the feast, the twelve fairies gave the little girl their best gifts: beauty and riches and goodness and much more.

Just as the eleventh fairy had finished her wish, there was a crash as the door swung open. It was the thirteenth fairy, whom everyone had forgotten.

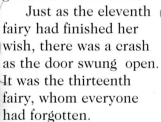

"Here's my present!" she screeched. "On her fifteenth birthday, the Princess will prick her finger on a spindle and die! That will teach you to forget me!"

As the guests looked at each other in horror, the twelfth fairy spoke.

"I can make the curse a little better," she said. "The Princess will prick her finger, but she will not die. Instead, she will fall asleep for a hundred years."

The years passed, and the Princess grew up to be clever, kind, and beautiful. On her fifteenth birthday, she woke up early.

Outside, she noticed a little door she had never seen before. She opened it and climbed eagerly up the stairs inside.

At the top of the stairs was a very old woman. Now the Princess had never seen anyone spinning before, for the King had banished all spindles from the kingdom.

"Would you like to try?" the old woman asked, holding out the spindle to the curious girl.

As she took the spindle, the Princess pricked her finger and at once fell asleep. At the same moment, everyone in the castle fell asleep as well—even the hunting dogs!

Many, many years later—exactly one hundred, in fact—a Prince happened to be passing the castle. It was so overgrown with brambles that you could only see the topmost turrets. But as he rode along beside the high, thorny hedge, it burst into bloom and opened to let the Prince through.

The Prince soon found himself in the small room where the Princess was sleeping. He could not resist bending to kiss her.

At that moment, the hundred years came to an end. The Princess opened her eyes, and saw a handsome young man, smiling down at her.

It was not long before the Prince and Princess were married. This time, the King was very careful indeed with his invitations!

THUMBELINA

There was once a woman who longed above everything else to have a little girl of her own. She went to a wise old woman to ask for advice.

"I want so much to have a little tiny girl to care for," she said.

"Take this barley seed," said the old woman, "and plant it in a pot."

So the woman
went home and
planted the seed.
It quickly grew into
a strong plant, with
one large bud. When
the flower opened,
the astonished
woman saw a little tiny girl, perfect in
every way, sitting in the middle.

Because she was no bigger than the
woman's thumb, she was called
Thumbelina.

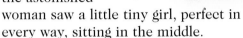

There never was a little girl who
was loved so much or cared for so well.
She had a walnut shell for a cradle and
rose leaves for a blanket.

As her mother worked around the house during the day, Thumbelina played on the table. She had a shallow dish of water, with a lily leaf in the middle, and she loved to sing as she rowed herself back and forth in the sunlight from the open window.

But one night a mother toad hopped through the window and saw the tiny girl in her pretty bed.

"She would make a beautiful wife for my son," thought the toad.

The toad carried the sleeping girl away and put her on a lily leaf in the middle of the river. The little girl was not frightened, but she did not want to marry the toad's son.

Thumbelina sat on her leaf and sobbed. A little fish popped up his head.

"You cannot marry that ugly old toad," he said.

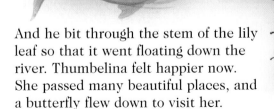

And he bit through the stem of the lily leaf so that it went floating down the river. Thumbelina felt happier now. She passed many beautiful places, and a butterfly flew down to visit her.

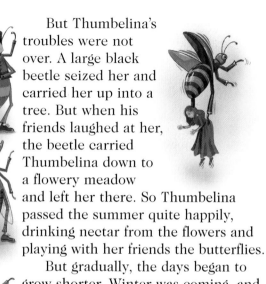

But Thumbelina's troubles were not over. A large black beetle seized her and carried her up into a tree. But when his friends laughed at her, the beetle carried Thumbelina down to a flowery meadow and left her there. So Thumbelina passed the summer quite happily, drinking nectar from the flowers and playing with her friends the butterflies.

But gradually, the days began to grow shorter. Winter was coming, and the nights were cold. Thumbelina knew that she could not survive the winter without a home to live in.

Just as the shivering girl began to lose hope, she met a busy little mouse. "You can stay with me, in my little house," said the mouse kindly.

Thumbelina was happy again, until the mouse's friend came to visit. He was a mole who lived underground, and he soon fell in love with Thumbelina.

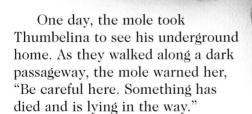

One day, the mole took Thumbelina to see his underground home. As they walked along a dark passageway, the mole warned her, "Be careful here. Something has died and is lying in the way."

It was a bird, but it was still alive! Thumbelina took care of the bird, and by spring, it was ready to fly away to join its friends. The little girl watched it fly away. She knew that when winter came again, she would have to marry the mole and live underground for the rest of her life.

Summer passed again, and Thumbelina stood and looked at the blue sky for the last time. Just then, a voice from above called to her. "Come with me!" It was the bird she had saved!

196

In no time at all, Thumbelina was sitting on the bird's back, soaring over fields and cities. At last the bird came to rest in a warm, sunny country, where orange trees grew and the air was full of the scent of flowers.

The swallow set Thumbelina down. You can imagine how surprised she was to see a little man, no bigger than herself.

"Welcome to my country," he said. "I am the Prince of all the flower people. We will call you Maia."

The little girl was happy at last.

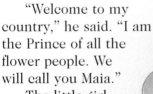

THE FROG PRINCE

Once there was a King who had seven beautiful daughters.

The youngest was the loveliest. On sunny days, she loved to play with her golden ball by a cool pool in the forest near the castle.

One day, when the Princess threw
her golden ball high into the air,
something dreadful happened. It fell …
SPLASH! … into the water.

"It is lost forever!" the girl cried.

"I could dive down and find
your ball," said a little green frog
by the pool, "if you would promise
that I could be your friend, share your
meals, and snuggle into your bed at night."

"Anything!" gasped the Princess.

But as soon as the frog had given her back the ball, the Princess ran back to the castle.

That evening, the King and his family sat down to supper. Just as they were about to start, there came a croaking at the door. The youngest Princess tried to ignore it.

But the King asked, "Who's there?"

Then the Princess explained about her promise.

"A promise is a promise, my dear," said the King.

So, although the Princess hated to look at him, the frog was allowed onto the table to share her supper.

After supper, the Princess tried to slip off to bed by herself.

"What about me?" croaked a little voice from the table.

"Remember what I said about promises," said the King.

The Princess unwillingly carried the frog to her bedroom and put him down in a corner.

"I'd much rather sit on your pillow," croaked the little creature.

Close to tears, the Princess dropped the frog onto her pillow.

At once, the little green frog turned
into a handsome, smiling Prince.

"Don't be afraid," he said.
"A wicked witch put a spell on me
that only a kind Princess could break.
I hope that we can still be friends,
now that I am no longer a frog."

A few years later, the Prince and
Princess were married, and you can be
sure that they invited some very
special little green guests!

THE EMPEROR'S NEW CLOTHES

The Emperor in this story was not interested in waging war or building castles, as most Emperors are. He simply loved clothes. It was well known that he spent most of the day trying on one costume after another to find which was most flattering to the (rather generous) royal figure.

One day there came to the court a pair of rascals intent on making a little money and living an easy life. They let it be known that they were weavers. "The cloth that we weave," they said, "is so fine, and its pattern is so intricate, that only intelligent people can see it."

Before long, the Emperor heard of this. "How very useful," he said to himself. "If I wore a suit of that cloth, I would be able to tell at once which of my ministers were too stupid and ill bred for their jobs." So he summoned the weavers before him.

"I would like a suit made of your famous cloth," he told them.

"No problem at all," replied the weavers. "If we could just take a few measurements. My, Your Highness has the figure of a man of twenty!"

Next the weavers ordered bales of costly silk and gold thread, to weave, they said, into their famous cloth. They had two looms set up in a comfortable room. All day they sat in front of the looms, pretending to weave.

The Emperor was anxious to see how his suit was coming along, but although he knew that he was the cleverest man in the land, he was just a little worried that he might not be able to see the cloth.

The Emperor thought long and hard until he had an idea.

"Summon my Chief Minister!" he cried. "He can report to me on the cloth the weavers are making for me."

Well, the Chief Minister couldn't see the cloth either. But he was worried that the Emperor might dismiss him, so he pretended it was wonderful.

Every day, the weavers called for more silk and gold. They packed this away in their luggage, ready for a quick getaway!

Soon the Emperor sent his Chancellor to inspect the work. Once again, the poor man could see nothing at all, but he did not want to lose his job. "It is beyond compare," he declared. "Your Highness will be really delighted."

The Emperor hurried to the weavers' room and flung open the doors.

He stopped dead. It was his worst nightmare! Only he, of all his court, was too stupid to see the wonderful cloth. His throat felt dry as he said, "This cloth is too beautiful for words!"

At the end of the week there was to be a Grand Procession. Naturally, it was expected that the Emperor would wear clothes of the famous new cloth. The weavers were busy night and day, cutting thin air with huge pairs of scissors, sewing with invisible thread, and pretending to sew on buttons.

On the morning of the Grand Procession, the Emperor stood in his underwear while the weavers helped him on with his clothes. By the time he had walked up and down a few times, he had persuaded himself that he could almost see the costume, and that it was very fine indeed.

So it was that the Emperor walked proudly out wearing only his second-best pair of royal underwear.

At first, there was a stunned silence from the crowd lining the streets. But everyone had heard that only clever people could see the clothes, so first one and then another spectator cried out, "Wonderful! Superb!" as the Emperor passed.

Sometimes, when everyone is making a lot of noise, there is suddenly a brief silence. In just such a moment, the voice of a little boy could be heard. "But Mother," he cried, "the Emperor isn't wearing any clothes!"

In that dreadful moment, the crowd realized that it was true, and they began to laugh. The Emperor ran in a most unroyal way back to the palace.

It is said that the Emperor never was quite so vain about clothes after that. And the two rascals? They had become as invisible as the Emperor's costume and were never seen again.

THE FISHERMAN AND HIS WIFE

One sunny day, a poor fisherman caught a very fine fish. He was just about to unhook it from his line, when the fish spoke!

"I am not really a fish but an enchanted Prince," he said. "Please put me back in the water."

"Of course," said the fisherman. "I wouldn't dream of eating a talking fish!" He put the fish back in the sea and went home to his wife.

The fisherman and his wife lived in a rickety old hut near the beach. It was in a terrible state! Everything was higgledy piggledy.

When the fisherman told his wife about the talking fish, she cried out, "You silly man! You should have asked for something for us in return. Go straight back and ask for a nice little cottage to live in."

So the fisherman went back to the seashore. The sun was hidden behind a cloud.

When the fish heard the man's request, he said, "Of course. Your wish is granted."

The fisherman went home. Where his hut used to be was a snug cottage.

At first all was well, but after a couple of weeks, the fisherman's wife said, "I deserve better than this. Go back and ask the fish to give us a castle. I want to be Queen!"

The next day, the fisherman did as she asked. The waves washed angrily against the shore, but the fish listened as before.

"Very well," he said. "Once more, your wish has been granted."

This time, when the fisherman trudged home, he found his wife surrounded by servants in an enormous castle. She seemed to be enjoying herself.

But only a few days later, the fisherman's wife said, "Being Queen is all very well, but I have been thinking...."

The fisherman's heart sank, as he set off for the seashore once again. The sea was very dark and stormy when he reached the water.

"Oh fish!" called the fisherman. "My wife wants to be Empress of the Earth and Sky."

"Go home," said the fish. "Your wife has all that she deserves."

And when he reached home, what did the fisherman find? Just a rickety old hut and his wife inside, complaining.

And the fisherman has not seen the talking fish from that day to this, although he looks for him all the time.

THE PRINCESS AND THE PEA

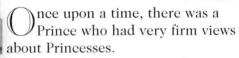

Once upon a time, there was a Prince who had very firm views about Princesses.

"Many of them are simply not Princesses at all," he said airily.

"My dear, whatever do you mean?" asked his mother the Queen. "We have met lots of charming girls."

"No. Princess Petunia spoke unkindly to her maid. Princess Pearl was *silly*. And Princess Petronella talked all the time and never listened to a word anyone else said. They weren't *real* Princesses. Real Princesses are ... well, they're ... that is, they seem ... oh, I don't know!"

"I do wish he could meet someone and settle down," sighed the King, as the Prince rushed from the room. "But how are we ever to be sure that a girl is a real Princess?"

"My dear," said the Queen, "just leave that to me."

219

That year, the Prince visited many countries and met many Princesses, but he found fault with every one of them. At last he returned home, sad and tired.

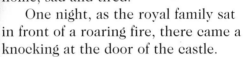

One night, as the royal family sat in front of a roaring fire, there came a knocking at the door of the castle.

"Some poor fellow is out in the storm," said the King. "We must let him in to warm himself."

The King
pulled open the
door himself.

Outside stood
a rain-drenched
figure. The King
had to peer more
closely to see that
it was a young girl
in a thin cloak.

"My dear
child," cried the
King. "Come in
at once!"

"My carriage
overturned, and I
was forced to go in
search of shelter,"
said the girl, as
she came inside.
"And you'd be
surprised how few
people are ready
to help a real
Princess knocking
on their door."

"Did you say a *real* Princess?" asked the King, looking at his wife.

"Of course," his visitor replied. "My father is a King."

"Well, well," said the King. "I wonder, have you met my son, the Prince?"

As the Prince came forward to greet the girl who made his heart stand still, the Queen hurried off to have her room prepared.

Half an hour later, the Princess was tucked up in her room.

The King could not wait to consult his wife.

"Well?" he whispered. "What do you think? The boy seems rather taken with her, but is she real?"

"We'll soon know about that," said the Queen. "I have put twenty mattresses on her bed. Below the bottom one I have placed a dried pea. Now we shall see what we shall see."

Next morning, the members of the royal family looked up eagerly as their visitor entered the room.

"My dear," said the Queen, "I hope you had a restful night."

"I'm afraid not," replied the girl, "although you made me so welcome and comfortable. I tossed and turned all night long, and this morning I am black and blue. It's as though there was a boulder under my mattresses."

At that the Queen beamed at her son. "Here," she said, "is a real Princess, my boy. Only a girl with truly royal blood would have skin so tender that she could feel a tiny pea through twenty mattresses. You have my blessing."

Luckily, it was soon discovered that the Princess had fallen as much in love with the Prince as he had with her.

They were married soon after, amid great rejoicing. And the royal museum still contains a rather wrinkled green exhibit. You can see it for yourself.

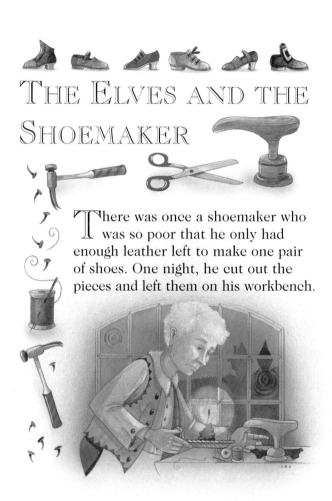

THE ELVES AND THE SHOEMAKER

There was once a shoemaker who was so poor that he only had enough leather left to make one pair of shoes. One night, he cut out the pieces and left them on his workbench.

The next morning, the shoemaker came downstairs to begin work. He was amazed to find that the leather had already been made into shoes!

The poor man couldn't understand what had happened, but he proudly put the shoes in his window. Within an hour, a very rich customer had seen the shoes and bought them.

"Now I have enough money to buy leather for two pairs of shoes," the shoemaker told his wife.

The next morning,
the shoemaker and
his wife could hardly
wait to creep down into
the workshop. Sure
enough, there on the
workbench were two
pairs of dainty shoes.
"I've never seen such fine
workmanship," gasped the shoemaker.

Once again, he had no trouble in
selling the shoes for a handsome price.
From that day onward, the
shoemaker's troubles were ended.
Soon his shop was busy all the time.

One day, near Christmas, the shoemaker's wife said, "I've been thinking that we should try to find out who has been helping us all this time."

The shoemaker agreed. That night, instead of going to bed, he and his wife hid behind the workbench and waited to see what would happen.

At midnight, the door opened and in danced two little men. They were dressed in rags, but they cheerfully sat down and began to sew. Before dawn, they slipped out into the street.

"So now we know," smiled the shoemaker.

"Surely, the least we can do to thank them is to make them some new clothes," said his wife. "And you could make them some little shoes."

A few nights later, the tiny presents were finished. The shoemaker and his wife hid as before.

Just after midnight, the little men appeared. At the sight of the clothes, they danced with happiness.

"Now that we
Are such fine men,
We need not come
To work again!"

they sang, and they skipped out of the shop, never to return.

THE SNOW QUEEN

There was once a mirror belonging to a magician. It made everything look ugly and twisted, no matter how beautiful it really was. One day, the mirror broke, and thousands of tiny pieces went flying across the world. Some flew into people's eyes and made everything look spoiled and dirty. Others were tiny sharp slivers that flew into people's hearts. They turned them to ice, so that they could not feel love and happiness anymore.

Meanwhile, a little girl and boy who
lived opposite each other were playing
happily high above the busy street.
Their houses almost touched, and
there were window boxes on the top
floor. In the summer, the little girl, who
was called Gerda, and the little boy,
who was called Kay, played together in
their tiny garden.

In the winter, when the windows
were shut, they watched the
snowflakes swirling through the
window like a flock of bees.

"There is a Queen of the
Snow just as there is a Queen
Bee," said Grandmother.
"She is the biggest snow-
flake, whirling in the storm."

That evening, when Kay was getting ready for bed, he peered through the window and saw one large snowflake landing on the window box. Before his eyes, it seemed to grow into a beautiful woman, dressed all in white. Kay knew that she was the Snow Queen but he turned back to his warm little bed.

The next day, when Kay and Gerda were playing outside, Kay suddenly gave a little cry.

"Oh," he said, "I just felt a sharp pain in my heart, as if something stabbed me, and it felt as though something flew into my eye, too. But I feel better now."

Tiny pieces of the magician's mirror were now lodged in Kay's eye and heart, which was turned to ice. Seeing Gerda's worried little face, Kay spoke coldly.

"What's the matter with you, Gerda? You don't look at all pretty like that. I'm going off to play with the other boys in the square."

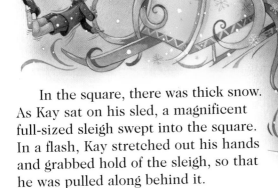

In the square, there was thick snow. As Kay sat on his sled, a magnificent full-sized sleigh swept into the square. In a flash, Kay stretched out his hands and grabbed hold of the sleigh, so that he was pulled along behind it.

As the sleigh flew over the fields,
the snow swirled thicker around Kay.
He began to be rather frightened.
     At last the strange sleigh stopped,
        and the white figure
           driving it stood up. Kay
             could see that it was
              the Snow Queen,
               dressed in a cloak
               of white fur.
                 Kay was no
                longer afraid but
               flew on with her
               in the moonlight.

Back in the city, little Gerda learned that Kay had disappeared. Everyone said that he must be dead, but Gerda could not believe that. As soon as spring arrived, she set off to find Kay in her new red shoes.

Gerda soon reached the countryside. Before long, she saw a large orchard, full of cherry trees, and an old woman wearing a straw hat, covered with flowers.

Gerda was glad to see a friendly face. Soon she had told the woman about Kay.

"I haven't seen him, but you can stay here and wait," said the woman.

In fact, the old woman really wanted
to look after a little girl just like Gerda.
She was careful to magic away all
the roses in her garden, so that
Gerda was not reminded of home.

But the old lady had forgotten about
her hat! One day, Gerda noticed that
one of the flowers on it was a rose.
"Oh, no!" cried the little girl. "I have
wasted so much time."

Without even waiting to put on
her shoes, Gerda ran
out of the garden. Her
feet were soon
sore, so she sat
down to rest
near a large raven.

"I may have seen Kay," said the raven, "but he has forgotten you. He thinks only of the Princess."

 "Is he living with a Princess?" asked Gerda.

Then the raven told her about a Princess who was very clever. She advertised for a husband, and before long, the castle was packed with young men lining up to see her. Unfortunately, when they came into her presence, all of them were too overcome to say a word, so she sent them away.

"But what about Kay?" asked Gerda.

Then the raven told how a boy who was not afraid of anyone came along and delighted the Princess by talking with her about all the things that interested her.

"Oh, that must be Kay. He is so clever," said Gerda. "I must see him!"

"I will see what I can do," cawed the raven, and he flew away.

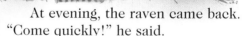

At evening, the raven came back. "Come quickly!" he said.

So Gerda hurried to the castle, where the raven's sweetheart was waiting. She crept up the back stairs. past swift shadows of horses and knights.

At last Gerda reached the Princess's room. There, sleeping soundly, was a young man. But it wasn't Kay!

Gerda was so disappointed that she burst into tears, waking the Prince and Princess. They felt sorry for the little girl and did what they could to help her. They gave her some new boots and a golden carriage, with footmen to take her on her way.

But Gerda's adventures were not over. As she passed in her carriage through a dark forest, some robbers jumped out. They could see that the carriage was worth a fortune. Those robbers might well have killed Gerda at once, but a little robber girl took her back to her home.

That night Gerda heard some wood pigeons cooing. "We have seen little Kay riding through the sky in the Snow Queen's sleigh."

The little robber girl's pet reindeer said quietly, "The Snow Queen has her summer palace near the North Pole. I know, for I was born near there."

The next morning, the little robber girl spoke to Gerda. "I heard everything last night," she said. "I will let the reindeer go if he will promise to carry you to Lapland to find Kay."

The reindeer jumped for joy, and Gerda climbed on his back. Night and day they flew through the forest and mountains, until the reindeer pointed out the beautiful northern lights and told Gerda that they had arrived in Lapland. There was a poor cottage nearby.

"You poor child," said the woman who lived there. "I'm afraid you have many miles to go yet."

Once again, Gerda and the reindeer flew over the snowy landscape, until they reached Finland. There they met a Finnish woman, who was a friend of the woman in Lapland.

"Can't you give Gerda some special magic, so that she can defeat the Snow Queen?" asked the reindeer.

"Gerda doesn't need any special magic," said the Finnish woman. "Her good heart is all the magic she needs. Kay is with the Snow Queen. He is happy there because he has a heart of ice and a fragment of the magician's mirror in his eye. Take Gerda to the edge of the Snow Queen's garden and put her down by a bush with red berries."

The reindeer
did as the Finnish
woman suggested,
although he was
sorry to leave Gerda
all alone in the cold
snow with her bare feet.

Almost at once, Gerda
was surrounded by
whirling snowflakes.
Some seemed to
threaten her but
others led her on.

245

And so it was that Gerda came at last to the Snow Queen's palace, with its walls of snow and doors and windows of bitter winds. Only Gerda's goodness kept her warm as she walked into a huge ice chamber.

There in the middle was little Kay, moving blocks of ice around as if he was trying to solve the hardest puzzle in the world.

Gerda ran forward. As she threw her arms around Kay, her warm tears of joy dripped onto his face and heart, melting the ice and washing away the slivers of mirror. The warmth gradually returned to his cheeks, and he too cried at the sight of his very best friend.

Outside, the reindeer was waiting. The children began their long journey home. At last they saw their own city stretching out before them.

Gerda and Kay were older and wiser, but in their hearts they were children still, and all around them was warmth and light and summer.

THE MUSICIANS OF BREMEN

Once there was a donkey who was old and tired. It became clear that his master would not keep him for much longer.

"The best thing for me to do," thought the donkey, "would be to go to Bremen and become a musician My braying has often been admired."

So early one morning, the donkey set off. On the way, he met a dog, sheltering by a wall.

"I am too old to go hunting with my master," growled the dog. "Now, he hardly feeds me at all."

"Come with me to Bremen!" laughed the donkey. "If I bray and you bark, we shall make fine music!"

And off they went. Before long, they met a cat, crouched on a roof.

"I am old and even the mice laugh at me," mewed the cat pitifully.

"Come with us and be a musician!" called the donkey and the dog. "Your voice is still strong and tuneful, you know."

Now the musicians made a loud noise as they went along, but when they passed by a farmer's barn, they heard a noise that was so loud, it drowned even their strange and wonderful singing.

"Cock-a-doodle-doo!"

"I am crowing," called the rooster. "because the farmer is having friends to dinner tonight. I'm very much afraid that I'm the main course!"

"Don't worry," the donkey replied. "I can think of a much better use for your voice. You just come along with us."

By the evening, the animals were
tired. They needed a place to sleep and
a fine dinner. At last, they saw the
lighted window of a little cottage.

When they reached it, the rooster
flew up and looked in the window.

"I can see four robbers,
sitting down to a delicious
meal!" he called.

"I have a plan," said
the donkey.

So the animals
climbed on each others'
backs. Then they went
right up to the window
and sang their music
at the tops of
their voices.

"It's a ghost!" cried one robber.

"It's a goblin!" cried another.

"It's a troll!" called the third.

"I want my mother!" sobbed the last robber.

In just a few minutes, the four animal friends had taken the robbers' places at the table and were enjoying a delicious meal.

Later that night, the animals slept soundly in the cottage. But the robbers crept back to see if the coast was clear. The animals were waiting.

As soon as the robbers were inside the cottage, the donkey cried, "Now!" and the animals attacked!

Well, those robbers ran away even faster than they had the first time, leaving the four friends in peace. The cottage was so charming that they never did reach Bremen, but they made time for their singing practice every day. And if you had ever heard them, you would know that the good people of Bremen had a very lucky escape indeed!

THE EMPEROR AND THE NIGHTINGALE

Long ago, the great empire of China had a mighty Emperor. His palace and his gardens were truly magnificent.

At the end of the gardens was
a wonderful forest, and beyond the
forest the deep blue sea stretched far
away. It was here, at the edge of the
water, that a nightingale had
made her home. Each
evening she opened her
heart and sang so
beautifully that even
the fishermen stopped
their work to hear her
liquid notes.

Many strangers
came to the palace
and every visitor
who heard the
nightingale's song
could not help
exclaiming,
"Everything here
is wonderful but
nothing compares to
the song of this magical bird."

When they returned home, some
of the visitors wrote books about
the place.

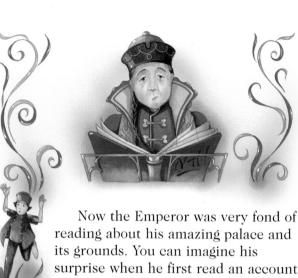

Now the Emperor was very fond of reading about his amazing palace and its grounds. You can imagine his surprise when he first read an account that rated the nightingale's song more highly than all his costly possessions.

"Why have I never heard the song of this bird, although she lives within my grounds?" he asked his courtiers. "Bring her to me tonight, for I must hear her sing."

The courtiers had never heard of the nightingale. They ran all over the palace, but they could find no one who had heard her.

The courtiers were almost at their wits' ends when they found a young maid in the Emperor's kitchens.

"I have heard the nightingale sing many times, when I go down to the shore to visit my mother," she said. "It is a truly wonderful sound."

The courtiers insisted that the kitchen maid lead them to the nightingale's tree. As they walked through the forest they heard a deep, booming sound.

"We have found the nightingale," they cried.

"No," said the maid. "It's a cow!"

The courtiers heard a bubbling, chirping sound.

"There's the nightingale," they declared.

"No, that's a frog!" said the maid.

Just then the nightingale began to sing. A ribbon of beautiful sound shimmered in the air. The kitchen maid pointed to a little brown bird on a branch.

"That is the nightingale," she said.

The courtiers were amazed, but they invited her to the palace that evening, as the Emperor had ordered. The whole court gathered that evening.

As the nightingale's first notes trembled in the air, tears rolled down the Emperor's cheeks. He had never heard anything so beautiful. The little bird was a great success.

After that, the nightingale had to live at the palace. She had her own golden cage and twelve servants. Twice a day, she was allowed to fly around a little, but one of the servants kept hold of a silken thread attached to her leg.

One day, a present arrived for the Emperor. It was a mechanical bird, made of gold and silver and precious jewels. When it was wound up with a golden key, the bird sang one of the nightingale's songs. It was a gift from the Emperor of Japan.

The mechanical bird sang very well, and always exactly the same song.

The Emperor was persuaded that this bird was the best.

The real nightingale took advantage of the commotion caused by the mechanical bird to fly through the window and back to its old, free life. Only the poor people, who were sometimes allowed to hear the mechanical bird, shook their heads and said, "No, there is something missing. This is not as beautiful as the real bird."

A year passed. One day when the mechanical bird was wound up with the golden key as usual, it merely said, "Krrrrr." The bird had sung so often that its mechanism was worn out. Luckily, the Court Watchmaker was able to repair the bird, but he warned that in future she must only sing once a year.

Several years passed, and the
people of China were shocked
to learn that their Emperor was
very ill. The courtiers were so sure
that he was about to die that
they began to pay court to the
man who would be the next Emperor.

In the middle of the night, the
Emperor was visited by fears and
phantoms. "Sing!" he begged the
mechanical nightingale at his side,
but there was no one to wind up the
metal bird, so it remained silent.

Suddenly, through the open window,
the Emperor heard a wonderful sound.

It was the real nightingale, singing her heart out. As she sang, the Emperor's fevered mind was soothed, and his illness left him.

"Thank you, little bird," he gasped. "You must remain in my palace and sing to me every day."

"No, My Lord," said the bird. "I cannot live in a palace, but I will come of my own free will and sing outside your window. And I will tell you what the poorest people in your land are thinking and feeling, which will make you the wisest Emperor who has ever lived."

The Emperor ruled for many more years, more wisely and well than ever before.

LITTLE RED RIDING HOOD

Once there was a little girl who lived on the edge of a huge forest. One day, her grandmother gave her a beautiful red cape with a hood. The little girl wore it all the time, so she was called Little Red Riding Hood.

One morning, Little Red Riding Hood's mother heard that the grandmother was not feeling well.

"Run along the forest path with this basket of food, Little Red Riding Hood," she said. "Your grandmother will feel better as soon as she sees you. But remember, you must go straight there and don't stop for anything."

Now Little Red Riding Hood had not gone very far, when out of the trees stepped a very large wolf!

"Why, Little Red Riding Hood," he said, "where are you off to?"

The little girl answered politely, "I am going to see my grandmother, but I'm afraid I cannot stop to talk." And on she went.

But when she was halfway to her grandmother's house, Little Red Riding Hood saw the wolf again. He said, "How nice it would be to take your grandmother some of the beautiful flowers that bloom by the path."

That did seem to be a good idea.

It was rather late by the time that Little Red Riding Hood knocked on her granny's door.

"Come in!" called a gruff voice.

Inside the cottage, Little Red Riding Hood tiptoed toward the bed.

"Why grandmother," gasped her granddaughter, "what big ears you have!"

"The better to hear you with!" croaked the invalid.

Little Red Riding Hood crept closer.

"Oh grandmother, what big eyes you have!" she cried in surprise.

"The better to see you with!" growled the figure in the big bed.

Little Red Riding Hood took one more step and had a dreadful shock.

"Oh grandmother, what big teeth you have!"

"The better to eat you with!" roared the wolf, jumping out of bed!

But just then, a passing huntsman rushed into the cottage. He chased the wolf right out of the cottage and into the trees.

Little Red Riding Hood heard a muffled sound from the cupboard. Bravely, she flung open the doors.

"Oh grandmother!" she cried with relief. "I thought you had been eaten! How are you feeling now?"

"I always feel better when I see you, Little Red Riding Hood," smiled her grandmother. "You must know that!"

THE UGLY DUCKLING

One sunny summer day, a mother duck sat on her nest.

It seemed to the duck that she had been sitting on her eggs for a long time. Then, one morning, she heard a tiny sound from one of her eggs. Out popped a fluffy duckling!

270

All at once, there were little sounds from more of the eggs. Before long, twelve fluffy little ducklings were cuddling up to their mother.

But one of the eggs—the largest of all—had not yet hatched. "How annoying," said the mother duck, and she settled down to wait a little longer.

Sure enough, a day or two later, there was a tapping from the egg. At last a funny little bird stood in the nest. He was the ugliest bird she had ever seen. He didn't look like a duckling at all.

"I'll push him into the water," said the mother duck. "If he cannot swim, I'll know he is a turkey."

But when she nudged the untidy bird out into the pond, he swam off quite happily. In fact, the duck felt 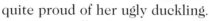 quite proud of her ugly duckling.

She set off to introduce her children to the other animals.

In the barnyard, the other ducks and the hens quacked and clucked in approval as the mother duck led her twelve little ducklings past. But when they saw the last duckling, they shook their heads and hissed.

"What a horrible bird!" they cried.

"He will grow into his feathers," replied the mother duck. She led her brood back to the pond.

As the ducklings grew, they loved
to waddle in the barnyard, shaking
their feathers. But the ugly duckling
soon dreaded the barnyard birds. They
pecked at him and called him names.

At last a morning came when the
little duckling could bear it no longer.
He ran away from the barnyard.

As night fell, he came, tired and hungry, to a wild marsh. In the morning, the wild ducks who lived there found a stranger among them.

"We've never seen a duck as ugly as you!" they laughed. "But you can live here if you like." The little duckling was still lonely, but at least no one bullied him. Then one day, as he swam by the bank, he suddenly saw a dog running through the reeds. All around the marsh were hunters and their dogs.

The duckling hid in the reeds all day, trembling with fright as shots whistled over his bowed head.

That night, he fled from his unsafe home.

The weather was growing colder when he came to a cottage and crept inside to escape the coming storm.

An old woman lived there with her cat and her hen. She let the duckling stay, but the animals were not friendly.

"You are no use at all," the cat and hen said.

At last, the duckling could bear the unkindness no longer. He wandered out into the world once more.

When the duckling came to a lake, he realized how much he had missed swimming. But winter was coming, and the nights grew colder.

One frosty day, a flock of beautiful white birds flew over the lake. He did not know that they were swans.

One morning, the poor duckling woke to find that he had become trapped in the frozen water. Luckily, a passing farmer freed him and carried him home to his family.

But the youngster was clumsy and knocked over dishes and pots. The farmer's wife angrily chased him from the house.

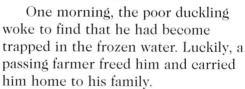

But gradually, the days became lighter. The bird found that his wings were stronger, and he could fly swiftly over the water. One afternoon, he caught sight of the beautiful white birds he had seen before far below.

As he landed, the swans rushed toward him, beating their wings. The bird bowed his head, waiting for their attack. As he did so, he saw his reflection. He wasn't an ugly duckling at all! He had grown up ... into a beautiful white swan! The other swans had come to welcome him.

"Oh look," cried some children who had come to feed the birds, "that new swan is the most beautiful one of all!"

Snow White and the Seven Dwarfs

One winter's day, a Queen sat sewing by an open window. Suddenly, she pricked her finger, and a drop of red blood fell on the snow below.

"I wish I could have a daughter with skin as white as snow, lips as red as blood, and hair as black as the window frame," sighed the Queen.

Before long, the Queen's wish came true. She called her baby Snow White, but sadly died soon after. The heartbroken King soon became lonely and found himself a new bride. She was very beautiful, but her heart was cold. Every day she looked into her mirror and asked:

"Magic mirror on the wall, Who is the fairest one of all?"

And the mirror would reply: *"O Queen, now I can truly say, You are the fairest one this day."*

279

But the day came when the mirror gave another reply.

*"O Queen, your time has fled away,
Snow White is the fairest one today."*

The Queen called for a huntsman.

"Take Snow White into the forest," she told him, "and bring me back her heart to show that she is dead."

The man did as the Queen had said, but when the moment came to kill the girl, he could not do it.

"Just leave me here," begged Snow White. "I promise never to come home."

So the huntsman took back an animal's heart and left the girl behind.

Snow White wandered through the trees for hours. Then, just when she thought she could go no farther, she saw a little cottage. No one came to answer her knock, so she tiptoed inside.

What a curious little house it was! On the table were seven little plates and seven little glasses. Poor Snow White was so hungry that she took a little food. Then, she climbed up the winding stairs to the bedroom.

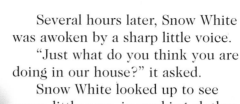

Several hours later, Snow White was awoken by a sharp little voice.

"Just what do you think you are doing in our house?" it asked.

Snow White looked up to see seven little men, in working clothes, standing around. She explained what had happened to her.

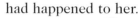

"And now," she said, "I have nowhere to go at all."

"Yes, you do!" chorused the little men. "You can stay here with us! But you must promise us never to open the door to a stranger."

282

So Snow White
stayed with the
little men. Her life
was very different
from the one she
had lived at home.
She longed for
someone to talk to during the long days.

Then, one fine morning, an old
woman, with a basket of pretty things,
knocked on the cottage door.

Snow White could not resist
talking to the woman through the
open window.

Snow White did not realize that her visitor was none other than the wicked Queen in disguise. For months, the Queen had been so happy that she did not consult her mirror. When she did, she had a terrible shock.

"O Queen, you'll not have your will,
For Snow White is the fairest still."

Raging through her kingdom, the Queen had hunted high and low for the missing girl.

"You are wise not to open the door to strangers, my dear," she smiled. "But to show that there are no hard feelings, please take this red apple as a gift from a new friend."

It seemed impolite to refuse. Snow White waved goodbye and took one bite.

When the little men returned from
their work that evening, they found
Snow White lying lifeless on the floor,
the apple still clutched in her hand.

"This is the work of the Queen,
I'm sure," cried one little man, sobbing.

Sadly, the little men took their
friend and placed her in a crystal coffin.

One morning, a young Prince rode by and saw the coffin and the lovely girl inside. He fell in love with her at once.

"Let me take her back to my palace," he begged, "where she can lie in state as befits a Princess."

The little men agreed that she deserved no less. Carefully, they helped the Prince to lift the coffin. But as they did so, the piece of apple caught in Snow White's throat was dislodged. She sat up and smiled at the Prince.

Snow White and her Prince lived happily ever after. And the wicked Queen was so eaten up with rage that she died soon after.

THE SHADOW

Once there was a writer who went to live in a hot country. Opposite his home was a house that seemed to be empty. But as he sat on his balcony one night, with the lighted room behind him, the man saw that his shadow seemed to be sitting on the opposite balcony.

"If only you could go inside for me and explore that house," said the man. And, you know, when he got up and went inside, the shadow did look as though it went into the house opposite.

The next morning, the man was astonished to find that he had no shadow at all! But by the time he returned to his home far away, his shadow had grown again.

One evening, there was a knock at the door. Standing outside was a very thin man.

"I suppose you don't recognize me," said the visitor, "I am your old shadow. I have become rich and wise since I left you."

Then the Shadow described how
he had entered the house opposite
and found that a goddess named
Poetry lived there.

"A great desire came upon me to
be a man," said the Shadow, "but I
had no clothes or money. The next
day—don't laugh!—I hid under the
baker woman's skirts and didn't come
out until nighttime. Then I ran here
and there, telling people truths about
themselves. And they were so afraid
that their friends would find out that
they gave me rich presents."

Then the Shadow took his leave.

A year passed, and the Shadow called on his old master again.

"Things are going even better for me," he said. "Look, I have grown quite plump. I feel like taking a trip and I would like a companion. Will you come with me—as my shadow?"

"That's crazy," said the man. "Of course not."

But the next year, the man became tired and ill. His friends told him that he looked like a shadow!

When the Shadow called again, the man agreed that a warmer climate would be good for his health. So he set off with the Shadow, and stayed at his side always, as a good shadow should.

At last the Shadow and his shadow reached a spa, where people go to get better from illnesses. Also staying there was a Princess. She talked to the shadow-man, and found him very intelligent. That made her think, "I will marry the man who is so amazing that even his shadow is wise."

As the wedding preparations were made, the Shadow said to the man, "Listen, I will give you money and a state coach if only you will always stay with me and never tell a soul that I was once your shadow."

"Never!" cried the man.

Then the Shadow ran quickly to the girl, looking shocked and pale.

"My shadow has gone crazy," he told her, "and thinks he is human!"

"It might be better," said the Princess, "if he was never seen again."

So that night, when the wedding took place, the Shadow's shadow was not there, and he has never been seen since.

THE TINDERBOX

One fine day, a soldier met a witch upon the road. "If you will climb into the hollow in that tree for me," she said, "you will be a rich man. All I want is an old tinderbox that you will find in there."

The soldier agreed. Inside the tree he found three chests of money, each guarded by a huge dog. He dealt with the dogs as the witch had said, filled his pockets with money, and, picking up the old tinderbox, climbed out again.

"You can cut off my head before I'll tell you why I want that old tinderbox," said the witch. So the soldier did!

After that, the soldier lived a fine life, but in a very short time, all his money was spent. Now he lived in an attic room.

One evening, the soldier felt in his pocket and found the old tinderbox. He thought he would use it to light his last candle. But as he struck three sparks from the flint, the dogs from inside the tree appeared before him. And the dogs were ready to do whatever the soldier asked, bringing him money, jewels, and other fine things.

Soon the soldier was as rich and happy as he had been before. One day, he heard of a beautiful Princess. Feeling curious, he sent the first dog to fetch her.

As soon as he saw the Princess, the soldier wanted to marry her. He kissed her and sent her home.

After that, the soldier could not help sending one of his dogs to fetch the Princess each night. But it was not long before the King and Queen tracked him down. He was quickly thrown into prison and sentenced to death.

"If only I had my tinderbox with me," said the soldier. He managed to give a message to a little boy outside his window, who ran off to fetch it.

With the tinderbox in his hand once more, the soldier knew that nothing could hurt him. He summoned the three dogs, who quickly over-powered the guards and chased away the King and Queen.

The people were happy to offer the throne to the Princess, and she was happy to accept it—and the hand of the handsome soldier whose face she had seen in her dreams.

RAPUNZEL

O nce there lived a man and wife who wanted very much to have a child of their own. But year after year passed, and they did not have a baby. Often, the woman would sit sadly looking out of the window, from which she could see the garden next door.

Now this garden was very beautiful, full of flowers and vegetables, but no one dared to enter it because it belonged to a witch. One day, as the woman looked out, she suddenly had a great longing to eat one of the lettuces growing below.

She looked so pale and anxious that her husband agreed to fetch her a lettuce.

That evening, the man crept over the garden wall. He was about to cut a lettuce when a voice cackled, "How dare you steal from me?"

It was the witch! Stuttering with fright, the man explained about his wife's great craving for lettuce.

"Very well," laughed the witch. "You may take a lettuce, if you will give me your firstborn child in return."

The man was so frightened that he agreed and hurried home.

And only a few months later, his wife gave birth to a beautiful baby girl. The witch made the man keep his promise. She took the child at once and called her Rapunzel.

The little girl grew quickly and became more lovely every day. The witch treated her like her own child, but when Rapunzel was twelve years old, the witch took her to a high tower and put her in a room at the very top. There was no door and no stairs—just a small window.

When the witch visited, she called out,

"Rapunzel,
Rapunzel,
Let down your hair!"

At this, the girl would lower her long, braided hair from the window, and the witch would climb up.

A few years later, a Prince came riding past and heard a beautiful voice singing from the top of the tower. He hid nearby and saw what the witch did.

As soon as the witch had gone, the Prince came out of his hiding place and called out,

"*Rapunzel, Rapunzel,*
Let down your hair!"

Thinking that the witch had returned, Rapunzel did as she was asked. She was astonished to see a tall, handsome young man climbing through the high window instead.

The Prince spoke kindly to the girl and, as she grew to know him, she grew to love him.

All went well until one day, when
the witch climbed into the tower,
Rapunzel spoke without thinking.

"Why is it, Mother, that you feel so
much heavier than the Prince does?"

The witch flew into a rage. She
took out some scissors and snipped off
Rapunzel's long braid. With her magic
powers, she banished the frightened
girl to a desert far away. Then she
crouched near the window and waited.

Before long, a voice drifted up:
"Rapunzel, Rapunzel,
Let down your hair!"

It was the Prince. Carefully, the witch lowered the braid of hair out of the window. As the Prince climbed into the room, she cried: "I wanted to keep my darling safe from such as you!" And she gave him a huge push.

The Prince fell like a stone into some bushes at the foot of the tower. He managed to stagger to his feet, but his eyes had been scratched by thorns, and he could not see at all. He stumbled away to a life of wandering.

Years later, the Prince came to the desert where Rapunzel was living. He heard her sweet voice, singing sadly.

"Rapunzel!" he cried, running forward.

The poor girl covered his face with kisses. As her tears of joy fell onto the Prince's eyes, he found he could see the girl he loved.

The Prince and Rapunzel returned to his kingdom, where they lived happily together for the rest of their days. The witch was never heard of again.

THE FIR TREE

Once upon a time, a little fir tree grew in a forest. All around him were beautiful trees, but the little fir tree was not happy. He wanted to be bigger.

"I wish I could be cut down," he said, "as the biggest trees are each year. Then I would travel over the sea. How wonderful!"

The little tree knew that the largest trees were made into the masts of ships. Each year at Christmas time, some smaller trees were cut down, too. "They are taken into people's homes," said the sparrows, "and decorated with toys."

That sounded even better to the little tree. He could think only of growing bigger. He cared nothing for his lovely home. All he wanted was to be grown up and gone.

And the very next Christmas, he was one of the first to be cut down.

Down in the town, the fir tree was chosen by a very grand family and carried back to their home. How proud he felt, covered with candles, ornaments, and presents.

That night, the children danced
around the tree and opened their
presents. It was such a pretty sight!

Next morning, some servants
removed the rest of the decorations
and put the tree away in a storeroom.
Only the golden
star on his highest
branch remained.

The tree was
lonely until some
mice came to talk
to him. They longed
to hear about his life in the forest.

"I suppose I was happy," said the fir tree. "But I did not feel it then."

Some months later, when the fir tree was yellow and dry, he was taken out into the yard.

The children stamped on his branches and broke them.

Then the tree realized how happy he had been in the storeroom, but he had not felt it at the time.

Before long, a servant came. He chopped up the tree for firewood. The poor tree was burned on the kitchen stove.

"How happy I was in the yard," he sighed.

Poor tree! All his life, he had always been wishing for something else, and never felt truly happy. Don't be like him, will you?

THE TWELVE DANCING PRINCESSES

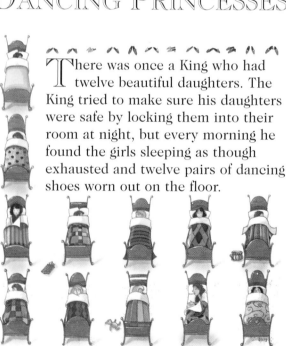

There was once a King who had twelve beautiful daughters. The King tried to make sure his daughters were safe by locking them into their room at night, but every morning he found the girls sleeping as though exhausted and twelve pairs of dancing shoes worn out on the floor.

The more the King thought about it, the more worried he became. At last he made a proclamation that whoever could solve the mystery might choose one of the girls to be his wife and become heir to the throne. But if, after three nights, the suitor was no nearer to the truth, then he must lose his life.

Several Princes came to try. But they all fell asleep outside the Princesses' room. And they all lost their heads.

One day, a wounded soldier passed through the kingdom. An old woman by the side of the road asked where he was going.

Joking, the soldier replied, "Oh, I'm going to find out what happens to the Princesses, night after night!"

The old woman answered, "That is not so difficult. You must simply leave the glass of wine that is given to you in the evening, for it is drugged. Then, put on this magic cloak. It will make you invisible."

When the soldier presented himself at the palace, he was given fine clothes to wear and shown to his bed in the hallway. The eldest Princess brought him a glass of wine, but he was careful only to pretend to drink it.

Then the soldier lay down and snored loudly to show that he was asleep.

As soon as they heard his snores, the Princesses put on brand new dancing shoes and their finest clothes.

Then the eldest Princess went to the head of her bed and pressed a secret panel. A passage-way opened up behind it. One by one, the Princesses went through.

Quickly, the soldier threw on the magic cloak and went after the girls.

But in his hurry, as he followed them down the stairs, he stepped on the youngest Princess's dress.

"What was that?" she cried.

"Don't be silly," the oldest Princess replied. "Come on!"

Before long, the Princesses reached the bottom of the stairs and came to an avenue of trees with leaves of silver and gold, gleaming in the moonlight.

The soldier broke a twig from the nearest tree.

"What was that?" The youngest Princess heard the tiny sound.

But the eldest Princess told her to be quiet.

"Hurry along," she said.

Next the Princesses came to an
avenue of trees with diamond leaves.
Once again, the soldier broke off a
twig as evidence.

"I heard something again, I'm sure
of it," whispered the youngest Princess.
But once more her sister silenced her.

At last they came to a lake where
twelve boats and twelve Princes were
waiting. The Princesses climbed in,
and the soldier joined the boat of the
youngest Princess, but of course, she
and her partner could not see him.

Across the lake stood a fine castle. From its open doors the sound of music streamed out over the water. Laughing and talking, the Princesses and their Princes hurried inside, where they were soon swept away by the waves of music.

By three o'clock in the morning, the Princesses' shoes were worn out. Saying goodbye to their Princes, they hurried back to their room in the palace.

This time, the soldier made sure he went ahead of them.

For two more nights, the soldier followed the Princesses. On the third night, he brought back a golden goblet.

"I have found the answer to the mystery," the soldier told the King, and he related everything that had happened to the dancing Princesses.

"And here," he said, producing the twigs and the goblet, "is my proof."

The King turned sternly to his daughters. "Is this true?" he asked.

The girls confessed at once.

"Then you may choose whichever one of these troublesome girls you would like for your bride," the King told the soldier.

"I am not so young myself," the suitor laughed. "I will choose the eldest, who was so certain that there was no one following. But I am sure that all of her sisters will gladly dance at our wedding!"

THE BRAVE TIN SOLDIER

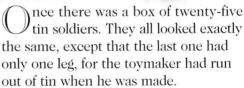

Once there was a box of twenty-five tin soldiers. They all looked exactly the same, except that the last one had only one leg, for the toymaker had run out of tin when he was made.

But the last tin soldier was just as brave as his brothers. At night, when the toys jumped up and played by themselves, he looked around and saw a fine toy castle with a lady at the door. She was very pretty, and she only had one leg, too!

"She would make a fine wife for me," said the tin soldier.

In fact, the pretty lady was a dancer, standing on one leg. Her other leg was tucked under her skirts.

Now the soldier was sitting on a jack-in-the-box! At midnight, the box burst open, and the soldier went flying over to the windowsill.

Next morning, when the windows were opened, he fell out! He landed on the pavement. Although his owner came to look for him, he went sadly back indoors when it started to rain.

When the rain ended, two boys saw the toy soldier and decided to put him in a paper boat.

At first all was well. The soldier stood up straight and strong, and the boat sailed off along the water running along the street. Then the water rushed into a drain, and the soldier found himself whirling into a dark cave.

"Halt! Who goes there?" cried a big water rat. The soldier, having no choice, rushed on.

Before he could do anything, the soldier's boat sank, leaving him floundering. Just at that moment, a passing fish opened its jaws and swallowed him!

Strangely enough, the fish was caught and taken to market. It was bought by the cook from the soldier's old home! In no time at all, he found himself back in the nursery.

The tin soldier looked longingly at the lady in the castle, and she looked longingly at him. But the soldier's adventures were not over. A little boy threw him into the fire. The little man stood and felt himself melting. At that moment, a rush of air sent the pretty lady flying into the fire to join him.

Next morning, when he raked out the fire, a servant found a tin heart— all that was left of the brave soldier and his lady love.

KING
THROSTLEBEARD

There was once a King who had a very beautiful daughter. But her heart was cold and proud. She laughed at her suitors and sent them away.

"Very well," said her father, "I will invite every eligible nobleman from far and near to a feast. Then you are sure to see someone that you like."

So every King,
Prince, Duke, Marquis,
Earl and Baron lined up
in the great hall, and
the Princess walked
up and down the rows,
like a general
inspecting his troops!

"Ho, ho, ho!
Look at his skinny
legs!" she laughed,
as she passed one
very learned Prince.

"Ha, ha, ha! He
looks like a frog!"
she giggled, as she
looked down at a
hardworking Duke.

At last she came to
a young King who was
charming in every
way. Still, there was
something about
his face that
reminded her of a
bright-eyed bird.

"I'll call you
King Throstlebeard,"
she chuckled. "I
couldn't possibly marry
someone so birdbrained! Ha, ha, ha!"
The Princess's father grew angry.
"You will marry the first beggar who
comes to the palace gates!" he said.

A few days later, a strolling player sat below the King's window and sang a haunting song. The King at once asked for him to be brought into the castle.

"Your singing has brought you a great reward," he said. "Here is my daughter. She shall be your wife."

And that is exactly what happened.

The Princess and her new husband were ushered out of the palace. They trudged along through some beautiful countryside, and the Princess wondered whose land could be so pleasing. Her husband replied, *"King Throstlebeard owns this. You could have lived in bliss."*

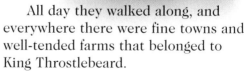

All day they walked along, and everywhere there were fine towns and well-tended farms that belonged to King Throstlebeard.

"I have been a fool," moaned the Princess. "If only I had married him!"

At last they stopped at a tiny hut.

"This is my home," the beggar told his new wife, "where you and I shall live together."

"But where do the servants live?" she asked.

"Servants?" chuckled the beggar. "You will be doing all the work around here, my dear."

So the Princess's new life began, but things did not go smoothly. She was no good at cooking or cleaning or washing the clothes. She could not make baskets or spin thread. Her husband grew angry.

"This is no good at all," he said. "We have to make a living. I'll buy some pots and you can sell them in the market. You should be able to do that!"

"But someone who knows me might see me!" wailed the Princess.

"So they might," replied her husband with a smile.

In fact, the Princess did well with her stall. She was so pretty that people were pleased to buy from her. She and her husband had enough money for some time. Then the beggar told her to take some new pots to market.

This time, things did not go so well. The Princess set up her stall on a corner. Before an hour had passed, a runaway horse crashed into the stall and broke every pot that she had. The Princess's husband was furious. "You are totally useless," he said.

"I cannot afford to keep you. But there is a post for a kitchen maid at the palace. They will feed you and you can bring home some scraps for me too."

So the Princess, who had once been so proud, had to work hard.

"It is my own fault," she admitted. "If I had not been so proud, I could have led a happy life."

At that moment, the King came out of the ballroom. To the Princess's horror, she realized that it was King Throstlebeard, whom she had rejected. Yet the King came straight toward the pretty girl and swept her into the dance.

"Don't be afraid," he said kindly. "I have taken on many forms, including the beggar whom you married. I see that you have learned to give up your pride and coldness. Now I am proud to make you my Queen."

From that day forward, the new Queen was the happiest woman in the world, and her kindness to everyone was known throughout the land.

THE WILD SWANS

Once there was a King who had eleven sons and one little daughter, called Eliza. They were very happy, although their mother had died. One day, the King married a new wife, who did not love children. She sent Eliza to live with a poor family and turned the boys into wild swans.

The years passed, and Eliza grew up to be both lovely and good. But the wicked Queen made sure that her husband did not want to see her.

The poor girl found herself homeless. Alone in the forest, she dreamed of her eleven fine brothers, handsome and grown up now.

The next morning, Eliza met an old woman on the path.

"Have you seen eleven fine Princes?" she asked.

"No," replied the woman, "but yesterday I saw eleven fine swans with crowns swimming in the stream."

Eliza followed the stream to the sea. At sunset, eleven swans with gold crowns came flying toward her. She watched until darkness came. Then each swan turned into a Prince once more. Eliza had found her brothers!

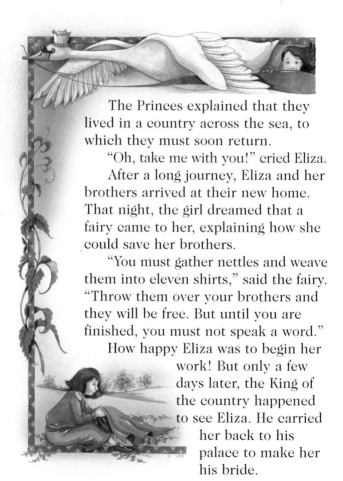

The Princes explained that they lived in a country across the sea, to which they must soon return.

"Oh, take me with you!" cried Eliza.

After a long journey, Eliza and her brothers arrived at their new home. That night, the girl dreamed that a fairy came to her, explaining how she could save her brothers.

"You must gather nettles and weave them into eleven shirts," said the fairy. "Throw them over your brothers and they will be free. But until you are finished, you must not speak a word."

How happy Eliza was to begin her work! But only a few days later, the King of the country happened to see Eliza. He carried her back to his palace to make her his bride.

Eliza grew to love the King, but still she worked on the nettle shirts. When she had nearly finished, the Archbishop persuaded the King  that she was a witch and should be put to death. Just in time, eleven swans flew down. Eliza threw the shirts over them, and the Princes appeared! The King was overjoyed as Eliza explained. But the youngest brother still had a swan's wing, for his shirt was not finished.

RUMPELSTILTSKIN

Once there was a miller who was not a very sensible man. One day, it was his turn to appear before the King and account for his year's work. At the end of the interview, the King asked about the miller's family.

The miller glowed with pride. "My daughter is not just beautiful," he said, "she is the cleverest girl in the kingdom."

"Really?" said the King. "Tell me, what can she do that is so clever?"

"She … can spin straw into gold!" blurted out the miller. He had said the first thing that came into his head.

The King was very fond of money. It seemed unlikely that the girl could do as her father said, but....

"Bring her to the palace," said the King. "And I mean right away!"

So the miller fetched his daughter. The King could not help noticing that she was very pretty. He took her to a small room, containing a spinning wheel and a huge heap of straw.

"Spin that into gold before dawn,"
said the King, locking the door, "or it
will be the worse for you."

The girl began to cry. Suddenly,
through her tears, she saw a strange
little man standing before her.

"I may be able to help you," he said.

The visitor's sharp little eyes twinkled greedily. "Your pretty glass necklace will be payment enough," he said, and at once he set to work.

While the poor girl cried herself to sleep, the little man worked at the spinning wheel. Before dawn, he had vanished as suddenly as he had arrived.

An hour later, the King was delighted to see a pile of golden thread where the straw had been.

"Tonight," he said, "I will give you a larger pile of straw."

That night, the little man again appeared to help the girl. This time, he took the ring from her finger as payment.

The King was a happy man. The next night, he showed the miller's daughter into an even larger room.

"If you complete your task again," he said, "I will make you my Queen."

But when the strange little man appeared, the poor girl sobbed, "I have nothing left to give you!"

The little man thought for a moment. "You can give me your firstborn child," he said.

What choice did the desperate girl have? Once again, the little man worked through the night.

The next day, there was great rejoicing in the castle. The King announced his wedding to the pretty girl who had won his heart. How proud the miller was!

A year later, the happy young Queen rocked her first child gently in her arms. Suddenly, the strange little man appeared.

"I've come to remind you of your promise," he said.

The Queen begged him to take her jewels instead of her child, but the little man shook his head.

"I'll give you one chance," he said. "If you can guess my name in three nights, you can keep your baby."

For the next two nights, the Queen tried every name she could think of—without success.

On the third night, a soldier came to her with an odd story.

"As I was riding through a wood," he said, "I saw a strange little man dancing around a fire and singing:

'The Queen can never win my game,
Rumpelstiltskin is my name!'"

347

That night, when the little man appeared, the Queen said, "Is your name Hibblehob?"

"No!" he yelled.

"Is it Grigglegreggers?"

"No, no, no!"

"Well, is it … Rumpelstiltskin?"

The little man went red in the face. He stamped his foot so hard that he disappeared right through the floor!

And, you know, no one has seen him from that day to this.

349

Cinderella

Poor Cinderella! All day long her two sisters yelled and scolded and made her do all the work. Although she had no fine jewels or pretty shoes, she was far more beautiful than they were, which made them dislike her even more.

One day a messenger from the palace invited all the young ladies from near and far to a ball to celebrate the Prince's birthday.

"Perhaps he will choose a bride at the ball!" said the sisters. They did not think of taking Cinderella.

After her sisters had left, Cinderella sat in front of the dying fire. "I wish that I could go to the ball," she sighed. Suddenly an old woman stood before her.

"I am your fairy godmother, Cinderella," she said. "And you *shall* go to the ball."

The fairy asked Cinderella to bring her a pumpkin. With a wave of her wand, she turned it into a beautiful golden coach. Then she turned six mice into six white horses to pull the coach. Finally, she waved her wand again and gave Cinderella a beautiful dress. "Now you are ready for the ball, my dear," she smiled.

"But remember, the magic only lasts until midnight. Before the clock strikes, you must hurry home," warned the fairy.

When Cinderella arrived at the ball in her golden coach, everyone in wondered who the beautiful stranger could be. The Prince himself led her to the ballroom and would let no one else dance with her all evening.

But as she whirled around the floor, Cinderella suddenly heard the great clock on the tower outside begin to strike. It was midnight!

"I'm sorry," she whispered and fled, leaving behind a glass slipper.

352

At home next day, Cinderella's sisters could talk only of the girl who had stolen the Prince's heart. Their complaints were interrupted by a royal messenger.

"The Prince has commanded that every girl in the kingdom must try on this slipper," he said. "And he has vowed to marry the one whom it fits."

"Let me try!" cried the first ugly sister. But her foot was too fat.

"My turn, I think," said her sister. But her foot was too long.

"Now it's your turn," said the messenger, turning to Cinderella.

"She's only a maid," laughed the sisters. "The slipper will *never* fit *her*." But the messenger was firm.

As Cinderella put on the dainty slipper, the Prince himself entered the house. At once he claimed her as his bride. So Cinderella and her Prince lived happily ever after.

Jack and the Beanstalk

"We shall have to sell our cow," said Jack's mother. "We have no more money."

So Jack set off to market with the cow, but on the way he met a stranger.

"Why walk all the way to market?" asked the man. "I'll take the cow now and I'll give you these magic beans in return."

Jack was delighted to have a handful of magic beans, but his mother was not so happy. She threw them out of the window. The next morning, a huge bean plant had grown beside the house.

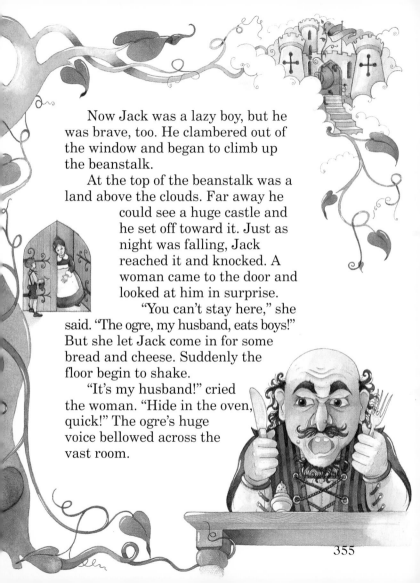

Now Jack was a lazy boy, but he was brave, too. He clambered out of the window and began to climb up the beanstalk.

At the top of the beanstalk was a land above the clouds. Far away he could see a huge castle and he set off toward it. Just as night was falling, Jack reached it and knocked. A woman came to the door and looked at him in surprise.

"You can't stay here," she said. "The ogre, my husband, eats boys!" But she let Jack come in for some bread and cheese. Suddenly the floor begin to shake.

"It's my husband!" cried the woman. "Hide in the oven, quick!" The ogre's huge voice bellowed across the vast room.

"Fee, fie, fo, fum,
I smell the blood
Of an Englishman.
Be he alive,
Or be he dead,
I'll grind his bones
To make my bread."

"That's just the soup ready for your supper," said his wife. Then the ogre shouted, "Bring me my hen!" His wife went out and fetched a white hen.

The ogre took the hen and cried, "Lay!" To Jack's amazement, the hen laid a golden egg! Again and again, the ogre ordered the hen to lay, until there were twelve golden eggs on the table. Then he fell asleep.

When he heard the ogre snoring, Jack jumped out of the oven, picked up the magic hen, and ran away.

He scrambled down the beanstalk, calling out, "Mother! Bring the axe!"

As soon as he was on the ground, Jack cut through the beanstalk with a mighty blow, and the ogre, who had been chasing him, fell to his death.

"Why Jack!" cried his mother. "That is the hen that the wicked ogre stole from your poor father. Now our troubles are over! I will never call you a lazy boy again, for you have saved us all."

So Jack and his mother lived happily ever after, and no more magic beans were ever grown in *their* garden!

The Gingerbread Man

Once upon a time a little old man and a little old woman lived in the country. One day, the little old woman made some ginger cookies. She had some dough left over, so she made a little gingerbread man, with three buttons and two eyes made of raisins and a smiley mouth made out of a cherry. But when the little old woman went to take him out of the oven, the gingerbread man jumped from the tray and ran right out of the door!

"Come back!" shouted the little old woman, running after him.

"Come back!" shouted the little old man, who was working in the garden.

But the gingerbread man called over his shoulder, "Run, run, as fast as you can! You won't catch me, I'm the gingerbread man!"

He ran down the garden path and out onto the road. As he ran, he passed a cow in a field.

"Stop!" mooed the cow. "You look good to eat!" And she ran after him. But the gingerbread man didn't stop for a single second.

"A little old woman and a little old man couldn't catch me and neither will you! Run, run, as fast as you can! You won't catch me, I'm the gingerbread man!"

In the next field he passed a horse. "Stop!" neighed the horse. "You look good to eat!" But the gingerbread man kept running. It was the same when he passed a rooster on a gate and a pig in a yard. The gingerbread man did not stop for anything ... until he came to a fast-flowing river.

"I can't swim," cried the gingerbread man. "What can I do?"

"Can I help you?" asked a quiet voice. It was a big red fox. "Jump on my back and I will carry you across."

The gingerbread man did as the fox said, and the fox swam into the river.

But soon the fox spoke again. "The water is deeper here. Climb onto my head and you will stay dry." The little man did so.

"The water is even deeper now," said the fox soon. "Climb onto my nose and you'll stay dry."

As soon as the gingerbread man did so, the fox tossed him into the air. The little man fell right into the fox's open mouth. When the little old man and woman came puffing along, only a few crumbs were floating in the water.

The Enormous Turnip

There was once a man who had a vegetable garden that was his pride and joy. One day he planted two rows of turnip seeds. In no time at all the plants were growing strongly. But one plant grew more strongly than all the rest! It grew and it grew, until it was the biggest turnip that anyone had ever seen.

At last the day came when the man decided to pull up his turnip. He grasped hold of the leaves and HEAVED … but he could not pull up the enormous turnip.

So the man called to his wife. "Please come and help me!"

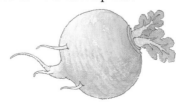

But the man and the wife together could not pull up the enormous turnip.

Just then a little boy walked past. "I'll help!" he said. But the boy and the man and the wife together could not pull up the turnip.

Next the boy's sister joined in. But it was no use.

A dog joined the chain. But the turnip did not move.

A cat pulled as well. But the enormous turnip stayed in the ground.

Finally, a little mouse helped the man and his wife and the boy and the girl and the dog and the cat to pull up the turnip. They heaved and they heaved and ... slowly ... the turnip came out of the ground. Phew! I believe they are eating it still!

Aladdin

Long ago a boy called Aladdin lived with his mother. They were very poor. One day, as Aladdin walked through the bustling market, he was greeted by a stranger, who held out two golden coins.

"At last I have found you!" cried the stranger. "I am your father's brother."

Aladdin and his mother welcomed the stranger as one of the family. On the third day, he said to Aladdin, "I have seen your eyes sparkle at my stories of faraway places. Come with me and I will show you something strange and wonderful."

Without hesitating, Aladdin followed the visitor out of the city.

In a wooded valley, the visitor lit a fire and threw some magic powder into it. He was not a kindly uncle at all, but a wicked wizard, who needed Aladdin for a special task.

The wizard showed the terrified boy a passageway.

"Go down the steps," he said, "but do not touch the gold and jewels that you see. In the furthest room, you will find an old lamp. Bring that lamp to me. But take this ring. It will protect you."

Aladdin did as he was told, but as he returned, holding the lamp, he heard the wizard plotting to kill him. Aladdin wrung his hands. In doing so, he rubbed the ring that the wizard had given him. All at once, a genie appeared.

"What is your will?" he asked.

365

"I'd like to go home," stammered Aladdin. At once it was done.

After that, the magic ring and the magic lamp meant that Aladdin and his mother lived very comfortably, but one day Aladdin caught sight of the Emperor's daughter and he fell in love with her.

Once again, he called upon the genie of the lamp to help. Aladdin and his bride were blissfully happy, but the wicked wizard managed to win back the lamp by trickery. With the help of the genie, he flew away to Africa, taking Aladdin's palace and the lovely Princess with him.

The genie of the ring and the Princess's cleverness defeated the wizard, and Aladdin and his wife lived happily ever after.

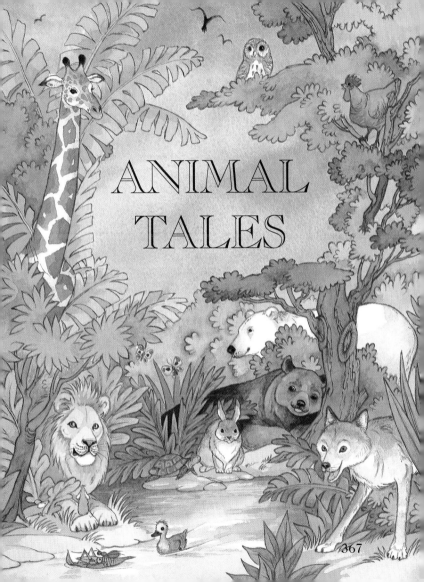

ANIMAL
TALES

The Three Little Pigs

Once there were three little pigs who decided to set off into the wide world to find homes of their own. "Remember," said their mother, "to watch out for the big, bad wolf!" The little pigs did not go far before they stopped to rest. Just then a man passed, carrying a load of straw. "With that straw I could build a strong, safe house," said the first little pig. And so he did.

Meanwhile, the other two little pigs had walked on until they met a farmer with a load of sticks.

"With those sticks I could build a strong, safe house," said the second little pig. And so he did.

Meanwhile, the third little pig had walked even further. Soon he met a workman with a cart piled high with fine red building bricks.

"With those bricks I could build a strong, safe house," said the third little pig. And that is exactly what he did.

369

That night the first little
pig heard a voice calling.
"Little pig, little pig, let
me come in!" It was the wolf!
"No, no, by the hair of my chinny
chin chin, I'll not let you in!"
"Then I'll huff, and I'll puff, and
I'll blow your house down!"
And the wolf huffed and puffed
and blew the house down. But the
little pig ran quickly to his brother.
The next night the two pigs in
the house of sticks heard a voice.
"Little pigs, little pigs, let me
come in!"
"No, no, by the hair of our chinny
chin chins, we'll not let you in!"

"Then I'll huff, and I'll puff, and I'll blow your house down!"

The wolf huffed and puffed and he blew down the house of sticks, but the two little pigs ran to their brother.

That night the wolf came again.

"Little pigs, little pigs, let me come in!"

"No, no, by the hair of our chinny chin chins, we will not let you in!"

"Then I'll huff, and I'll puff, and I'll blow your house down!" And he huffed and puffed but he could not blow the house down.

The wolf was *cross*. "I'll climb down the chimney!" he said.

But the third little pig put a huge pot of water on the fire. When the wolf leapt down the chimney, he landed with a splash. And that was the end of him!

371

The Hare and the Tortoise

There was once a hare who was very proud of his running. "No one is as speedy as me!" he cried. "Would anyone like to race?"

"No thanks!" laughed the other animals. "We know you can run faster than any of us."

But one little voice piped up politely behind him. "I'll give you a race if you like, Mr. Hare," it said.

The hare turned around in surprise. Standing before him was a wrinkly old tortoise.

"Oh my!" replied the hare. "You make me tremble, *Mr.* Tortoise."

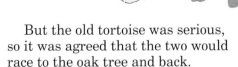

But the old tortoise was serious, so it was agreed that the two would race to the oak tree and back.

"On your marks! Get set! Go!" yelled the squirrel.

In a couple of seconds, the hare was nearly out of sight. The tortoise set off in his usual slow way.

When he reached the tree, the hare was so confident that he sat down to rest. But he soon fell fast asleep!

An hour later, he woke up and heard cheering in the distance. Leaping to his feet, he ran as fast as his legs would carry him, but the tortoise's head bobbed over the line a whisker before the hare's.

"Being quick on your feet is a fine thing, Mr. Hare, but slow and steady wins the race," said Mr. Tortoise.

373

The Fox and the Goat

One hot summer, a fox wandered into an abandoned garden. Before he knew what was happening, he had tumbled into an old, deep well.

There was not very much water in the well, so the fox was quite safe at the bottom, but the sides were smooth and straight. The fox soon realized that he could not climb out.

The fox was beginning to think that he would never escape, when a foolish face looked over the top of the well.

"Hello down there!" boomed a voice. It was a goat.

The cunning fox at once saw his chance.

"My friend," he called, "come and share this lovely cool water with me!"

So the silly goat jumped into the well and drank the water. But before long, even the goat began to wonder how they could get out.

"Easy, my friend," said the fox. "Put your front feet as high up the wall as you can. I'll climb onto your back and jump to the top. Then I'll help you."

The goat did as the fox said. In seconds, the fox was out of the well and away. The poor goat was stuck.

Like the well, the moral of this story's deep: remember to look before you leap.

Puss in Boots

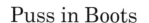

Once there was a miller with three sons. When he died, he left his mill to the eldest and his donkey to the middle son. To the youngest he left the cat that caught mice at the mill.

"How are we going to make a living?" sighed the youngest son.

"Don't worry," said the cat. "Give me a pair of your old boots and a bag." The miller's son did as Puss asked. The clever cat put some lettuce leaves in the bag and left it in a field. When a little rabbit came out and nibbled at the leaves, Puss ran out and caught it.

Then the cat set off to see the King.

"Your Majesty," said Puss, "Please accept this present of a fine rabbit."

The King was amused by the cat. "Who is your master, Puss?" he asked.

"My master is the Marquis of Carrabas," said the cat grandly.

One day the cat told his master to go for a swim in the river. "And you must pretend," he said, "that you are the Marquis of Carrabas."

When the King came past in his carriage, he saw Puss running around.

"Oh Your Majesty," cried Puss, "my master's clothes have been stolen!" (In fact, Puss had hidden them himself in some bushes nearby!)

377

In no time at all, the King had
sent for a fine suit of clothes for the
young man. When he was dressed,
he was invited to ride in the royal
carriage and be introduced to the
King's daughter, the Princess.

Meanwhile Puss was running along
the road ahead until he reached a
huge castle. Bravely, he walked
straight up to the ogre
who owned it.

"I've heard you can do
magic, Your Hugeness,"
said Puss. "I should so
love to see some."

The ogre laughed and turned himself into a lion!

"Hmm," said Puss, "but could you become something very small?"

In a second, the ogre turned himself into a mouse. At once, Puss pounced!

When the King arrived, Puss was ready. "Welcome to my master's home, Your Majesty."

The King was very impressed and so was the Princess. Before long she and the miller's son were married and they and the clever cat lived happily ever after.

Town Mouse and
Country Mouse

Once upon a time there was a busy little mouse who lived in the country. One morning, his cousin, who lived in the nearby town, came to visit him.

"The country is so peaceful," said Town Mouse with a sigh. But that night, Country Mouse was awakened by a forlorn little figure standing by his bed.

"Oh cousin," said Town Mouse.
"I'm so frightened. There are horrible
rustling and scurrying noises outside."

Country Mouse listened. "Those
are just ordinary country sounds," he
said. "You'll soon get used to them."

The next day, Country Mouse was
busy as usual, picking berries and
seeds to store for the winter. But
Town Mouse did not want to work.

In the afternoon, Country Mouse
made a picnic for his cousin. But
Town Mouse was frightened of the big
cows and horses in the field.

"Come back to town with me," he
said to his cousin. "You'll love it there."

So Country Mouse set off with
Town Mouse. After a long day's
journey, they reached the big house
where Town Mouse lived.

"Isn't it splendid?" yelled Town
Mouse. But Country Mouse could not
hear him because of the traffic.

The mice had all the food they
could eat from the pantry. But
Country Mouse found it too rich.
"I think I'll go to bed now," he said.

But he didn't get a wink of sleep!
The streetlights kept him awake all
night. And next morning, Town
Mouse had to save his cousin from a
hungry cat! It was the last straw.

"Thank you for having me to
stay," said Country Mouse, "but I'm
going home to my old oak tree!"

Good Morning, Farmer!

One morning, a farmer set out from the farmhouse on his rumbling red tractor.

"Cluck, cluck!" said the hens. "Where are you going?"

"Oink, oink!" snuffled the pigs. "Are you going to market?"

"Baa, baa!" bleated the sheep. "Are you off to the hay field?"

"Honk, honk!" called the geese. "Are you going far?"

"Woof, woof!" barked the dog. "Aren't you taking me too?"

"And *where* are you going?" they snuffled and honked and barked.

But the farmer just smiled and chewed on a straw.

"Meow, meow!" cried the cat. "Are you going to collect something?"

"Quack, quack!" said the ducks. "Are you going to the river?"

"Moo, moo!" called the cows. "Are you going to the dairy?"

And all together they meowed and quacked and mooed. "Where *are* you going? Please tell us *now*!"

The farmer gave a smile as wide as the farm.

"With all this noise, I should think you could guess," he chuckled. "I'm off to town to buy some earplugs, of course!"

385

The Ant and the Grasshopper

Long ago on a sunny hillside, there lived an ant and a grasshopper. The grasshopper was a handsome insect with a glossy green coat. All day long he sat in the sun and made music, filling the hillside with his summery sounds.

"I don't believe that winter will ever come!" he chirruped.

The ant was small and dark. She bustled about every day, collecting grass seeds to store in her nest. "

"Oh yes, it will!" she said.

But soon the leaves began to fall from the trees. It grew colder and colder. At last one day, feathery flakes of snow began to fall across the hillside.

The ant was snug in her nest under a stone. She had enough food for the winter. Outside she heard a faint sound. It was the grasshopper.

"Dear Ant," he croaked. "Please give me some food."

But the Ant was firm. "I'm sorry," she said. "I need this food for my family."

A thick layer of snow settled over the hillside, and the grasshopper was heard no more.

The Little Red Hen

Once there was a little red hen who found some grains of wheat. She carried them off to the farmyard.

"Who will help me to plant this wheat?" she asked.

But the cat said, "Not I!"

And the rat said, "Not I!"

And the pig said, "Not I!"

"Then I shall plant it myself," said the little red hen. And so she did. By the end of the summer the wheat was high and golden.

"Who will help me harvest my wheat?" asked the little red hen.

"Not I!" said the cat.
"Not I!" said the rat.
"Not I!" said the pig.

"Then I shall harvest it myself," said the little red hen. And so she did.

When the little red hen asked for help to take her wheat to the miller and to the baker, it was the same story. She did it all by herself and baked the flour into beautiful brown loaves.

Then she said, "Who will help me to eat my bread?"

"I will!" said the cat.

And "I will!" said the rat.

And "I will!" said the pig.

"Oh no," said the little red hen. "I shall eat it all myself." And so she did.

The Elephant and the Mouse

Once there was a huge elephant who lived in the forest. He crashed along on his big, flat feet.

But one morning, as the elephant trampled across a clearing, he heard a tiny squeaking sound.

"Oh please," said a tiny voice, "please be careful! You're standing on my tail!"

Trapped by the elephant's foot was a very small mouse.

"I'm sorry," said the elephant. "I'll be more careful in the future."

From that day, the elephant
always made sure that he was
not stepping on a tiny creature.
In fact, he was so busy being
careful that he did not notice the
hunters creeping up on him. Soon
he was trapped in the hunters' net.

As he sat there sadly, the
elephant was astonished to hear
a tiny voice.

"One good turn deserves
another," squeaked the little mouse.
And she gnawed through the net.
With a happy trumpeting sound,
the elephant broke free!

The moral of this story is
clear. If you help other people,
they will help you!

The Wolf and the Seven Little Kids

Once upon a time there was a mother goat who had seven little kids. One day the mother goat had to go into the forest to find some food, but before she went, she spoke seriously to her seven children. "My dears," she said. "While I am gone you must not open the door to anyone, especially Mr. Wolf. You can always tell when he comes calling, because he has a gruff voice and rough, hairy paws."

392

The little kids promised that they would be very careful, and their mother set off for the forest. Before long there came a knock at the door.

"My dears," said a gruff voice, "it's your mother. Let me in!"

"You are not our mother," said the kids. They could see the wolf's paws on the window sill. "She doesn't have a gruff voice like you. Or rough, hairy paws! Go away!"

At this Mr. Wolf was very angry.

393

He hurried home and drank a honey drink to make his voice soft. Then he dipped his paws in white dough and ran back to the cottage.

The little kids heard his soft voice and saw his smooth white feet. "It *is* mother!" they cried and opened the door. In a flash, the wolf gobbled them all – except one.

When the mother goat came back, the little kid who had hidden told her everything.

"Right," she said, "I saw that old wolf asleep outside. Hurry!"

She crept up to the sleeping wolf and made a tiny hole in his fat tummy. Out jumped the six little kids! Then their mother filled the hole with stones and sewed it up.

When the wolf woke up, he staggered to the well for a drink, but his tummy was so full that he fell in and was never seen again.

The Owl and the Pussy Cat

The Owl and the Pussy Cat went to sea
In a beautiful pea green boat:
They took some honey, and plenty of money
Wrapped up in a five pound note.
The Owl looked up to the stars above,
And sang to a small guitar,
"O lovely Pussy, O Pussy, my love,
What a beautiful Pussy you are,
You are, you are!
What a beautiful Pussy you are!"

Pussy said to the Owl, "You elegant fowl,
How charmingly sweet you sing!
Oh! Let us be married; too long we have tarried:
But what shall we do for a ring?"
They sailed away, for a year and a day,
To the land where the bong-tree grows;
And there in a wood a Piggy-wig stood,
With a ring at the end of his nose,
His nose, his nose,
With a ring at the end of his nose.

"Dear Pig, are you willing to sell for one shilling
Your ring?" Said the Piggy, "I will."
So they took it away, and were married next day
By the turkey who lives on the hill.
They dined on mince and slices of quince,
Which they ate with a runcible spoon;
And hand in hand, on the edge of the sand,
They danced by the light of the moon,
The moon, the moon,
They danced by the light of the moon.

Androcles and the Lion

Long ago there lived a young man called Androcles. He was owned as a slave by a rich Roman merchant, who treated him cruelly. One morning, Androcles ran away.

By midday, Androcles was too tired to run any further. He looked desperately for somewhere shady to hide and caught sight of the opening to a cave. Weak with hunger and exhaustion, he crawled inside.

Inside the cave, Androcles was terrified to see a fearsome lion. But the lion had a thorn in his paw and was suffering badly. Androcles could not bear to see such pain.

Bravely, he pulled out the thorn, and the lion padded softly away.

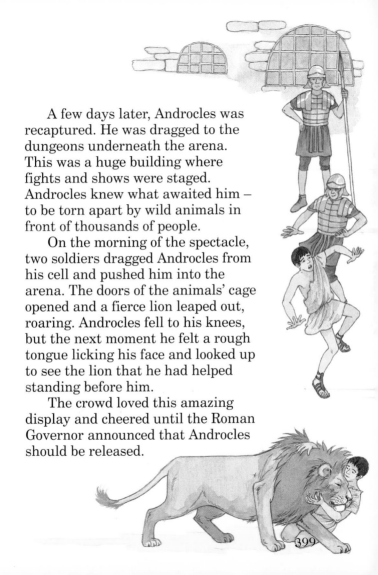

A few days later, Androcles was recaptured. He was dragged to the dungeons underneath the arena. This was a huge building where fights and shows were staged. Androcles knew what awaited him – to be torn apart by wild animals in front of thousands of people.

On the morning of the spectacle, two soldiers dragged Androcles from his cell and pushed him into the arena. The doors of the animals' cage opened and a fierce lion leaped out, roaring. Androcles fell to his knees, but the next moment he felt a rough tongue licking his face and looked up to see the lion that he had helped standing before him.

The crowd loved this amazing display and cheered until the Roman Governor announced that Androcles should be released.

Peter and the Wolf

Once there was a little boy who lived with his grandfather. His grandfather said, "Peter, you must never, ever go out of the garden and into the meadow. For the wolf may come out of the forest and eat you!"

Peter promised, but one sunny morning, he opened the garden gate and walked out. High in a tree was a little bird.

"Have you seen the wolf today?" asked Peter.

"No," sang the bird. "But you must
warn that duck who has followed you."

The duck wanted to swim in the
pond in the meadow. "Come and join
me," she shouted to the bird.

"No," chirruped the bird. And she
fluttered up and down on the bank.
But she did not see a cat, creeping
through the grass behind her.

"Look out!" called Peter,
as the cat sprang, and
the bird flew safely up
into a tree.

"Thank you, Peter,"
she sang.

A little later, Peter's grandfather came out into the garden. He heard laughing coming from the meadow.

"Peter!" he shouted. "Come back into the garden at once!" Peter promised not to open the gate again.

Meanwhile, out in the meadow, a dark, shadowy shape crept out of the forest. It was the wolf!

The bird and the cat escaped into a tree. But the duck was too slow, and the wolf swallowed her whole!

Peter had seen everything from the garden. He thought of a clever plan to save the cat and the bird.

Peter found a piece of rope and climbed up onto the garden wall.

"Fly around the wolf's head and make him dizzy," he called to the bird. Distracted by the bird, the wolf did not see Peter dangle the rope down until he was firmly caught by the tail!

Just then some hunters came out of the forest. A grand procession took the wolf to the zoo.

"Quack! Quack!" Inside the wolf the duck stamped her feet with joy to think that she would soon be rescued. No wonder the poor wolf wasn't feeling very well!

Noah's Ark

Long ago there was a very good man called Noah. He always tried to do what was right.

One day, God spoke to Noah. "I am going to wash away all the wickedness in the world, but you will be saved," He said. "I want you to build a huge boat, an ark, and put on it your wife and family and two of every kind of animal on earth."

Noah did as God had said, although passers-by jeered at him.

"You're welcome to join us if you like," Noah said, but the foolish people roared with laughter.

When the ark was finished, Noah called his sons and their wives and asked them to help him round up two of every kind of animal on earth.

"*Every* kind?" his youngest son asked.

"*Every* kind," said Noah firmly.

So two by two, the animals were led into the ark, and God shut its great doors.

405

Almost at once, black clouds
rolled across the sky and heavy rain
began to fall. Once it started, it just
didn't stop. Day after day it fell in a
steady stream. The ark
gave a lurch and a roll.

"We're floating!" cried
Noah.

For forty days and
nights the ark floated on
the floods. At last the
rain stopped.

"The floods will begin
to go down. We must find
land," said Noah.

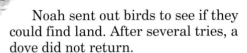

Noah sent out birds to see if they could find land. After several tries, a dove did not return.

"She has found a place to build a nest," said Noah. The next day, with a bump and a jolt, the ark settled on the top of a mountain.

Joyfully, Noah and his family and all the animals climbed out of the ark.

"Well done, Noah," said God. "I promise that I will never again destroy the world that I have made." And He made a rainbow, arching from the earth to the heavens, to remind us of His promise.

Chicken Licken

One day as Chicken Licken was walking along, an acorn fell on his head. "Oh my," said Chicken Licken. "The sky is falling in! I must go and tell the King."

So Chicken Licken set off. On the way he met Henny Penny and Cocky Locky.

"I am going to tell the King that the sky is falling in," said Chicken Licken.

"Then we shall come too," said Henny Penny and Cocky Locky.

So Chicken Licken
and Henny Penny
and Cocky Locky set
off to find the King.
On the way they
met Ducky Lucky and
Drakey Lakey.
"Where are you off
to?" they asked.
"The sky is falling in," cried
Chicken Licken, "and we are going to
tell the King."
"Then we shall come too," said
Ducky Lucky and Drakey Lakey.
So Chicken Licken, Henny Penny,
Cocky Locky, Ducky Lucky and
Drakey Lakey set off to find the King.

On the way they met Goosey
Loosey and Turkey Lurkey.
"Where are you off to?" they asked.
Chicken Licken told them.
"Then so shall we," said Goosey
Loosey and Turkey Lurkey.
So Chicken Licken, Henny
Penny, Cocky Locky, Ducky
Lucky, Drakey Lakey and
Goosey Loosey set off to
find the King.
On the way they
met a fox.
"Where are you
going?" asked
Foxy Loxy.

"The sky is falling in and we are going to tell the King!" they cried.

"Then follow me," said Foxy Loxy. "I know the way." So Chicken Licken, Henny Penny, Cocky Locky, Ducky Lucky, Drakey Lakey, Goosey Loosey and Turkey Lurkey followed Foxy Loxy. But he led them to his den, and his family ate them for dinner!

So all those foolish birds never did get to see the King. But then the sky didn't fall in either!

Among the Leaves

Who is that chirruping,
among the leaves?
"I am," said a sparrow.

Who is that
buzzing, among
the leaves?
"I am," said a fly.

Who is that shining,
in a pool among
the leaves?
"I am," said a fish.

Who is that scuttling,
among the leaves?
"I am," said a beetle.

412

Who is that hooting,
among the leaves?
"I am," said an owl.

Who is that croaking,
among the leaves?
"I am," said a raven.

Who is that singing,
among the leaves?
"I am," said a lark.

Oh, there is so much
to be heard and seen,
Among the leaves
so green, so green.

A Present for Percy

Sometimes it is difficult to find a present for a friend. Percy's friends had that problem every Christmas.

That pig did nothing all day but watch television! He didn't read books and he didn't play games. In fact, most days he didn't even get dressed! No, Percy just sat in his chair and watched and watched...

414

One year, Percy's friend Bella had an idea.

"Here's an exercise tape, Percy," she said.

And Percy did watch that tape, over and over again. But he never once stirred from his chair!

Perhaps this year, Percy will change his ways. For no one has bought him anything!

To Santa

415

The Three Billy Goats Gruff

Once there were three billy goats called Gruff. They lived in the mountains, searching for the fresh, green grass they loved to eat.

One day the three billy goats Gruff stood on a hillside and looked across a river. There was the freshest, greenest grass they'd ever seen. The goats trotted along the river until they came to a bridge.

"The bridge may not be very strong," said the smallest billy goat. "I will go first to make sure."

Now under the bridge lived a wicked old troll. When the smallest billy goat Gruff's hooves went *trip, trap* on the wooden planks, the troll peeped over the edge of the bridge.

"Who's that trip-trapping across *my* bridge? I'm a troll and I'm going to eat you for my dinner!" he roared.

But the goat replied, "I'm the smallest billy goat Gruff. My brother will be tastier than me."

17

So the troll let the smallest billy goat Gruff go trip-trapping on across the bridge and onto the fresh, green grass on the other side.

Next the middle-sized goat began to cross the bridge. When he was in the very middle, the ugly old troll popped up again.

"Who's that trip-trapping across *my* bridge?" he roared. "I'll eat you up!" But the middle-sized billy goat replied, "Wait for my brother. He is much bigger!"

So the greedy troll let the middle-sized goat go.

Now the biggest billy goat Gruff had seen everything that had happened and he smiled to himself. His big hooves went *trip, trap* on the wooden planks. This time the troll jumped out and stood on the bridge.

"Who's that trip-trapping on *my* bridge?" he shouted. "Dinner at last!"

"I'm the biggest billy goat Gruff of all," came the reply. He lowered his horns and CHARGED!

With a great roar, the troll flew up into the air and down into the river below. The water carried him away, never to be seen again, and the billy goats Gruff lived happily ever after.

The Sly Fox and the Little Red Hen

Once there was a little red hen who had a neat little house in the woods. Her home kept her safe from the sly fox who lived nearby.

One morning the little red hen went into the woods to collect some sticks for her fire. She didn't know that as she worked, the sly young fox ran quickly into her house and hid behind the door.

When the little red hen hurried home with her sticks, the sly young fox jumped out! Squawking with terror, the little red hen flew up to the roof and perched on a rafter.

The sly young fox laughed. "You can't escape from me so easily, Little Red Hen!" he said, and he began to chase his own tail around and around the room. The little red hen watched until she became so dizzy that she dropped off her perch.

That was just what the sly young fox had planned. He put the little red hen into a sack and set off for home.

On the way, the fox lay down near some rocks and went to sleep. When she heard him snoring, the little red hen made a hole in the bag and wriggled out. Then she quietly put some large stones into the sack. Finally, she tiptoed away and ran all the way back to her snug little home.

Soon the sly young fox woke up and set off once more. The little red hen felt heavier than before!

When he reached his den, the fox's mother was delighted.

"The water is boiling, my clever boy," she said. "Throw her in at once."

With an enormous splash, the stones fell into the boiling water. The water splashed all over the two foxes and gave them such a fright that they ran away, leaving the little red hen to live happily ever after.

CHRISTMAS STORIES AND RHYMES

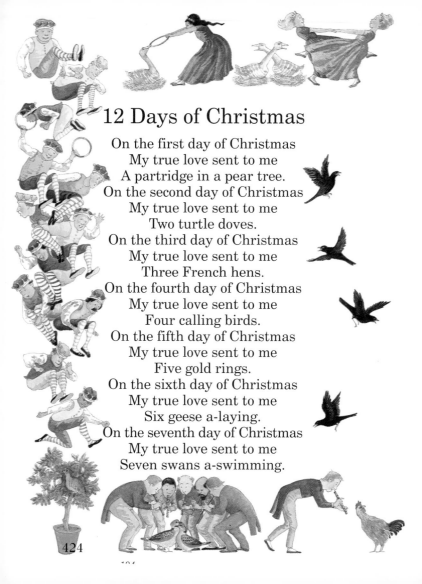

12 Days of Christmas

On the first day of Christmas
My true love sent to me
A partridge in a pear tree.
On the second day of Christmas
My true love sent to me
Two turtle doves.
On the third day of Christmas
My true love sent to me
Three French hens.
On the fourth day of Christmas
My true love sent to me
Four calling birds.
On the fifth day of Christmas
My true love sent to me
Five gold rings.
On the sixth day of Christmas
My true love sent to me
Six geese a-laying.
On the seventh day of Christmas
My true love sent to me
Seven swans a-swimming.

On the eighth day of Christmas
My true love sent to me
Eight maids a-milking.
On the ninth day of Christmas
My true love sent to me
Nine drummers drumming.
On the tenth day of Christmas
My true love sent to me
Ten pipers piping.
On the eleventh day of Christmas
My true love sent to me
Eleven ladies dancing.
On the twelfth day of Christmas
My true love sent to me
Twelve lords a-leaping, eleven
ladies dancing, ten pipers piping,
nine drummers drumming, eight
maids a-milking, seven swans
a-swimming, six geese a-laying,
five gold rings, four calling birds,
three French hens, two turtle doves
and a partridge in a pear tree.

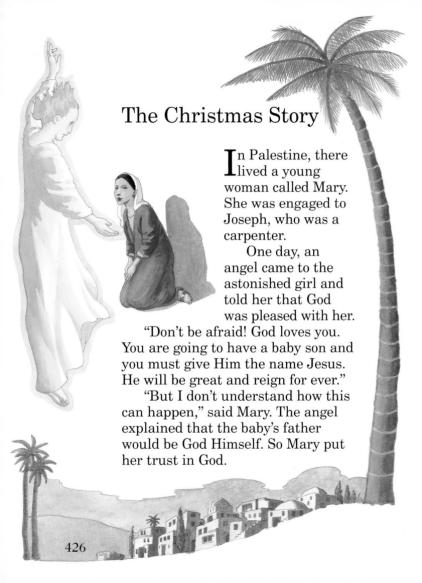

The Christmas Story

In Palestine, there lived a young woman called Mary. She was engaged to Joseph, who was a carpenter.

One day, an angel came to the astonished girl and told her that God was pleased with her.

"Don't be afraid! God loves you. You are going to have a baby son and you must give Him the name Jesus. He will be great and reign for ever."

"But I don't understand how this can happen," said Mary. The angel explained that the baby's father would be God Himself. So Mary put her trust in God.

When the baby was soon be born,
Mary had to travel with Joseph to
Bethlehem to take part in a census.
But none of the inns had any room.
At last a kind innkeeper let them
stay in his stable. That night, Mary's
baby, Jesus, was born. Mary laid
Him in a manger, on the hay left for
the animals to eat.

427

On the hills around Bethlehem, some shepherds were watching their sheep. Suddenly a bright light shone on them and a voice told them not to be afraid. The voice told the shepherds of the birth of Jesus. The trembling shepherds saw that the sky was filled with singing angels. At once, the shepherds hurried to Bethlehem to see the baby Jesus.

Far away, wise men also saw the bright star. They knew it was a sign that a great King had been born.

The wise men followed the star. They thought that the new King would be born in a palace, and they visited King Herod in Jerusalem. But Herod asked them to tell him when they found the King. He planned to kill the baby as soon as possible.

At last the star stopped above the stable where Jesus lay. The wise men gave Him gifts of gold, frankincense and myrrh. Then God sent dreams to the wise men and Joseph, warning them of Herod's plan. The holy family fled to Egypt and safety.

Silent Night

Silent night, holy night,
All is calm, all is bright
Around yon Virgin,
Mother and Child,
Holy infant,
So tender and mild.
Sleep in heavenly peace,
Sleep in heavenly peace.

Silent night, holy night,
Shepherds quake at the sight;
Glories stream from heaven afar,
Heavenly hosts sing hallelujah.
Christ, the Redeemer, is born,
Christ, the Redeemer, is born.

The Little Match Girl

One cold and bleak New Year's Eve, a poor little girl, trying to sell matches to buy herself a crust of bread to eat, shivered in a doorway. No one wanted to stop as they walked quickly by. Some did not even see her bare feet and ragged clothes.

When the streets began to empty and the lamplit windows called home the last passers by, the little match girl struck one of her precious matches to try to keep warm.

431

It seemed as though a glowing fireplace appeared before her. With a little cry, she stretched her frozen feet toward it, but the match went out and the fire disappeared.

With shaking fingers, the little girl struck another match. Now it seemed as though she could see through the wall of the house opposite. There was a table piled high with good things to eat, but as she stretched out her hands, the match went out and the vision vanished.

With tears in her eyes, the little girl struck a third match. Now she seemed to be inside the room, sitting under a candlelit tree.

432

As the tree's lights faded, the little girl lit her last match. She saw her beloved grandmother smiling at her.

"Please let me stay with you for ever!" cried the poor girl.

At that the old lady gathered her into her arms and carried her gently into the sky.

The next day, passers by found the little girl. She had gone to a better home than any on Earth for her New Year.

433

Good King Wenceslas

One snowy night, good King Wenceslas looked out of his castle and saw a poor man, carrying a bundle of sticks through the snow.

"Who is that man and where does he live?" the King asked his page. The boy replied that he was a peasant, whose home was at the foot of the mountain, on the edge of the forest.

"Bring me food and drink and some logs for his fire," said the King. "We will go visiting."

So the King and his page went out into the blizzard. Soon the page called out, "Sire, I cannot go any further!"

"Walk in my footsteps," replied the King. "Look, we have arrived!"

The poor man and his family had a wonderful Christmas. They were not the last to bless the name of that saintly King.

Jingle Bells

Dashing through the snow
In a one-horse open sleigh,
O'er the fields we go,
Laughing all the way.
Bells on bobtail ring,
Making spirits bright.
What fun it is to laugh and sing
A sleighing song tonight!

Jingle, bells! Jingle, bells!
Jingle all the way!
Oh, what fun it is to ride
In a one-horse, open sleigh – hey!
Jingle, bells! Jingle, bells!
Jingle all the way!
Oh, what fun it is to ride
In a one-horse open sleigh!

The Best Present

"I want a *big* truck," said Charlotte, "and I want some more carriages for my train, and I want a box of crayons, and I want...." The list went on for some time, so that Charlotte's mother, who was feeling quite tired, stopped listening very soon. Thank goodness Charlotte's father was out in the town now, picking up the present that they had planned for their daughter.

"Now Charlie," said her mother, "sit down with me and listen. I really must tell you...." But just then Charlotte's dad arrived home with a huge package. "No looking, Charlie!" he cried, puffing upstairs.

"Can we play horses?" demanded Charlotte.

"Not now, Charlie. I don't really feel like it," said her mother, "and anyway, I still want to have a quiet talk with you."

But Charlotte didn't want to talk quietly. She wanted to run and jump and yell because that's how she felt with Christmas coming – *tomorrow*!

Much, much later, after quite a lot of running and jumping and yelling, Charlotte went to bed at last.

"Now if you hear any rustling and bustling in the night, you MUST NOT open your door," smiled her dad.

The next morning, Charlotte ran into her parents' room and suddenly stood quite still with her mouth open.

"Oh Charlie!" laughed her mother. "I don't think I've ever known you to stand so quiet and still for so long! Here's a present for all of us that came a bit earlier than I expected."

"This is the best present I've ever had!" said Charlotte. And, you know, she didn't even look at the big box waiting for her on the floor.

Deck the Hall

Deck the hall with boughs of holly,
    Fa la la la la la la la la,
'Tis the season to be jolly,
    Fa la la la la la la la la,
Fill the mead cup, drain the barrel,
    Fa la la la la la la la la,
Troll the ancient Christmas carol.
    Fa la la la la la la la la.

See the festive board before us,
    Fa la la la la la la la la,
Strike the harp and join the chorus,
    Fa la la la la la la la la,
Follow me in merry measure,
    Fa la la la la la la la la,
While I sing of beauty's treasure,
    Fa la la la la la la la la.

Fast away the old year passes,
    Fa la la la la la la la la,
Hail the new, my lads and lasses,
    Fa la la la la la la la la,
Laughing, dancing, all together,
    Fa la la la la la la la la,
Heedless of the wind and weather,
    Fa la la la la la la la la.

Deck the hall with boughs of holly,
    Fa la la la la la la la la,
'Tis the season to be jolly,
    Fa la la la la la la la la,
Fill the mead cup, drain the barrel,
    Fa la la la la la la la la,
Troll the ancient Christmas carol.
    Fa la la la la la la la la.

Traditional carol

Baboushka

Once there was an old woman called Baboushka who lived all by herself in a wooden hut in the forest. The nearest house was many miles away. Although Baboushka was very poor, she was happy.

One winter's night, as Baboushka sat sewing by her fire, she heard three knocks on her wooden door.

On the doorstep stood three very fine and important looking men.

"Come in, come in. You are very welcome on such a cold night," said Baboushka.

As she busied herself making the tea and finding some food, Baboushka asked the strangers where they were going.

"We are following a star that will lead us to the place where a new Prince has been born," said one man. "We do not know where it will stop."

"Who is this new Prince that you seek?" asked the old woman.

"He is a holy child," said the second man. "He is the Christ child, who will reign forever."

Baboushka's eyes widened as the third man showed her the precious gifts that had been brought for the new baby. "I wish I could see this holy child," she said.

"Then why not come with us?" the three men replied. "You are welcome."

"No, no," said Baboushka, sadly. "I am too old to go on a journey."

Soon the snow eased a little and the three men set off once more.

All night long, old Baboushka thought of the Christ child.

"I *will* go," she said. She packed a bag of toys for the new baby and set off across the snow. Poor Baboushka! She had waited too long. She could not find the three strangers. Some say that she is still searching, giving gifts to poor children on her way.

I Saw Three Ships

I saw three ships
Come sailing in,
On Christmas Day,
On Christmas Day,
I saw three ships
Come sailing in,
On Christmas Day
In the morning.

And they sailed into
Bethlehem,
On Christmas Day,
On Christmas Day,
And they sailed into
Bethlehem,
On Christmas Day
In the morning.

Traditional carol

The Real Reindeer

Across the ice of
the Arctic Circle,
a brown shape moved
slowly. It was a real
reindeer, separated from
his herd in a snow storm.

One night, as he gazed
into the sky, the reindeer
saw something strange flying
toward him. With a crash, it
landed on the snow a few yards
away, and a jolly man called out.

"Need a job?" the man asked. "One of my reindeer left at short notice."

The reindeer cleared his throat. "Er, well, the fact is ... I've never learned to, er, *fly*."

The old man was doubled up with laughter. "Don't worry," he said. "I give on-the-job training. Come on!"

So the reindeer took his place with the others. "Hurry up!" cried the man in red, climbing into the sleigh. "This is a busy night for me! Three, two, one ... lift off!"

All that night, the sleigh flew over towns and villages, delivering presents. At last, the old man pulled off his cap. "Just one more present to deliver," he said.

Soon, the sleigh flew over a snowy landscape once more. "Will this be okay?" asked the old man. "There seems to be a few reindeer here already. Do you mind?"

"Mind? It's my *family*!" cried the reindeer joyfully. And he ran off to join them.

"Well, that's the last present delivered," chuckled Santa Claus. "See you next year!"

The Christmas Mouse

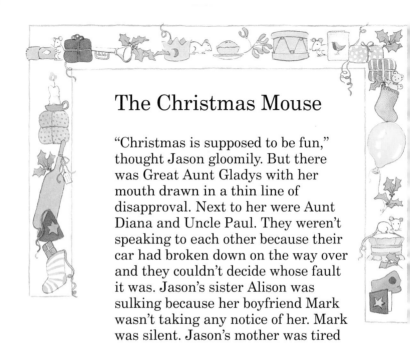

"Christmas is supposed to be fun," thought Jason gloomily. But there was Great Aunt Gladys with her mouth drawn in a thin line of disapproval. Next to her were Aunt Diana and Uncle Paul. They weren't speaking to each other because their car had broken down on the way over and they couldn't decide whose fault it was. Jason's sister Alison was sulking because her boyfriend Mark wasn't taking any notice of her. Mark was silent. Jason's mother was tired out and his dad was fast asleep.

Jason couldn't bear it any longer.

"Perhaps everyone would like to see my presents," he suggested.

"If there's something *quiet* you can bring, get that," said his mother.

So Jason went to his room and carefully lifted his new white mouse, Snowy, from her box.

Nothing had changed down in the dining room. Jason walked across to Great Aunt Gladys, his eyes on his cupped hands. That was why he didn't see the stool that she was resting her feet on.

In the confusion, everyone yelled together. But Jason was loudest, "Where's Snowy?"

There was a silence for a moment. "What?" asked everyone at once.

"Snowy, my mouse," explained Jason.

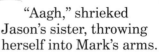

"Aagh," shrieked Jason's sister, throwing herself into Mark's arms.

"I *love* mice," cried Great Aunt Gladys, on her hands and knees.

"I'll catch it in my bag," yelled Aunt Diana.

"Stand clear, we need team-work," shouted Uncle Paul.

Five minutes later, the crisis and the gloomy silence were over. Mark and Jason's sister were giggling on the sofa. Uncle Paul beamed at his wife. "Using your bag was *brilliant!*"

"You organized everyone so well," she smiled back.

"I'm going to give that mouse the biggest hunk of cheese it's ever seen," said Jason's dad. "Merry Christ*mouse*, everyone!"

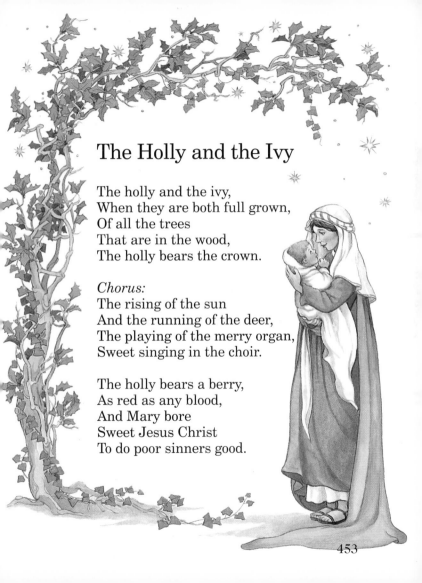

The Holly and the Ivy

The holly and the ivy,
When they are both full grown,
Of all the trees
That are in the wood,
The holly bears the crown.

Chorus:
The rising of the sun
And the running of the deer,
The playing of the merry organ,
Sweet singing in the choir.

The holly bears a berry,
As red as any blood,
And Mary bore
Sweet Jesus Christ
To do poor sinners good.

The Little Christmas Tree

Many years ago, deep in a forest, a little fir tree grew in a small clearing. All around it were huge trees, their tops reaching up toward the sky.

One day a truck with lots of men in it came along. It was time for the big trees to be felled and taken to the sawmill to be made into timber.

"All these are to go – except this little one, of course," said the foreman.

454

That night the little tree felt sad.

"I am sorry that you are going to be cut down," he said to the big trees.

The trees rustled their branches.

"Don't worry about us," they said. "Our tall, smooth trunks will be used to make all kinds of interesting things. But you will just be thrown away."

Then the little tree was even more sad. He gazed up at the night sky. "This is the last time that I shall see the stars," he thought.

The next morning, the big trees were felled. But the foreman did not pull the little fir tree up. He dug very carefully around him and lifted him, with a ball of earth around his roots.

Then he put the little tree in his truck and drove to his home. Three little children ran out and laughed.

"You've brought the Christmas tree!" they cried. "It's a lovely one!"

Today the little tree stands, tall and strong, near the house, and at night his branches almost seem to touch the stars.

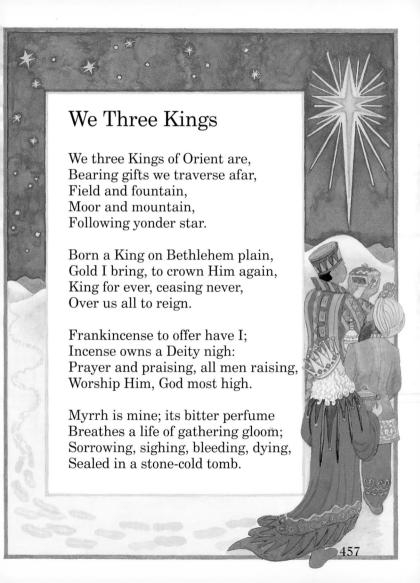

We Three Kings

We three Kings of Orient are,
Bearing gifts we traverse afar,
Field and fountain,
Moor and mountain,
Following yonder star.

Born a King on Bethlehem plain,
Gold I bring, to crown Him again,
King for ever, ceasing never,
Over us all to reign.

Frankincense to offer have I;
Incense owns a Deity nigh:
Prayer and praising, all men raising,
Worship Him, God most high.

Myrrh is mine; its bitter perfume
Breathes a life of gathering gloom;
Sorrowing, sighing, bleeding, dying,
Sealed in a stone-cold tomb.

457

The Runaway Present

It was Christmas Eve, and all the Christmas presents were piled up under the tree. There were big ones and small ones, long, thin ones and round, fat ones.

The clock struck twelve in the quiet room. Suddenly, the pile of presents began to move slightly.

"Let me through! Excuse me! Please let me through!" said a voice.

At last a small present, wrapped in red and green, with a big bow on the top, struggled out of the pile.

It ran out of the door and off down the path, leaving tiny footprints in the snow.

All night long, the little present kept running. An owl sitting in an old oak tree looked down at the hurrying present below. Silently, he swooped down and picked up the present in his beak, carrying it back to his branch to examine it.

"Please don't eat me," cried the present. "I wouldn't taste good, honestly I wouldn't. And I'm in a hurry, you see."

"Too whoo!" hooted the owl. "Where to?"

459

"I got mixed up in the pile of presents under the Christmas tree. I should have been sent to the children's granny in the next town. She'll be so disappointed if I don't arrive. I really must try to get there by myself."

"Too whoo!" said the owl. "Well, flutter my feathers, that's the strangest story I've ever heard. If you give me directions, I'll carry you into town."

So the owl flew off through the trees, carrying the present in his beak.

Soon they arrived at the children's granny's house.

"Here I go!" said the present, jumping through the cat flap. "Bye!"

When you are unwrapping your presents next Christmas, look carefully to see if one of them is a little bit out of breath, for that will be a very special present indeed.

461

The Christmas Carol Mystery

"It's a mystery," said Vikky, "and someone must find out their secret." She was talking about Christmas carols. Every year two groups of singers went around the town, collecting money for charity. And every year the group from St. Mary's Church Choir, who sang like angels, collected less money than the group from the Youth Club, who made a really horrible noise, even when they sang easy carols.

462

"What we need," commented Janine, "is a spy! One of us should go around with the Youth Club."

"My cousin Jemima is coming to stay for Christmas," said Vikky. "They don't know her."

So that was what happened. Jemima went along to the Youth Club and volunteered.

Jemima reported back to St. Mary's.

"I think you should go out singing on Wednesday night," she said. "Before the Youth Club have a chance to do it first."

The St. Mary's Choir spent all Wednesday evening trudging the streets, calling at every house. They collected a lot of money.

On Thursday, Jemima set off to join the Youth Club group.

"All right, team," said Gary, their leader, as they reached the first door. "One, two, three ... Jingle bells..."

And there began the most awful noise that Jemima had ever heard. In seconds, a face appeared at the door and the noise stopped. "Another carol, sir?" asked Gary politely.

"No, no!" cried the man, throwing money at the choir.

And so it went on. Time and again, the Youth Club were paid handsomely to go *anywhere* else!

Jemima enjoyed herself so much that she never did tell her cousin how the Youth Club Choir succeeded. After all, there was room for both of them. You won't either, will you?

The Christmas Snowman

"It's the same every year," muttered the snowman. "Those children give me an old hat and a moth-eaten scarf and then forget about me. That man in the red coat and beard comes along and it's as if I don't exist. Ugh."

The next day the snowman wasn't any happier.

"I can feel a thaw in the air," he grumbled. "Drip, drip, my toes are melting already."

The snowman was still grumbling that night when there was a wooshing in the sky and a sleigh pulled by reindeer swooped down onto the snow.

"Oh no," said the snowman gloomily. "It's that man in red. What on earth does *he* want?"

The old man strolled up to the snowman.

"Could you look after this bag of presents for me?" he asked. "I'll leave the children a note to say that you've got it."

"It'll be safe with me, sir," said the snowman, proud to have a *real* job at last. He didn't close his eyes all night, as he guarded the bag.

467

In the morning, all the children from the house across the street came running over the snow to find their presents. Their dad came too with his video camera and filmed them opening their gifts.

"Fame at last!" thought the snowman. "That man in red never stays around long enough to become a star like me. Poor guy. I am lucky after all. The children would miss me as much as him if I were not here."

Well, almost!

In the Bleak Midwinter

In the bleak midwinter
Frosty wind made moan,
Earth stood hard as iron,
Water like a stone;
Snow had fallen, snow on snow,
Snow on snow,
In the bleak midwinter,
Long ago.

What can I give him?
Poor as I am?
If I were a shepherd,
I would bring a lamb;
If I were a wise man,
I would do my part;
Yet what I can I give him –
Give my heart.

Christina Rosetti

469

Mrs. Muddle's Present Puzzle

One morning, Mrs. Muddle said, "I will *not* get into the kind of muddle I did last Christmas. I will shop *early*."

All day she was busy shopping. Then she wrapped up *everything*. There was a train set for her nephew Jimmy, a scarf and hat for her brother Sam, a cookbook  for stern Aunt Susan, sensible socks for Great Uncle Harry, roller skates for little Susie and a microscope for Susie's big brother, Tom.

Then Mrs. Muddle hid the presents under the bed.

On Christmas Eve, Mrs. Muddle took out her presents. But she hadn't put any labels on them! There wasn't time to undo the presents and wrap them up again, so Mrs. Muddle just had to guess.

On Christmas day, Mrs. Muddle looked out and saw Great Uncle Harry roller-skating past.

"Best present I've had in years! Thanks!" he cried.

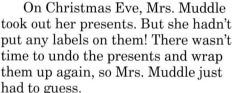

A second later, little Susie came past on *her* new roller skates.

"These socks are great! It doesn't hurt at all when I fall over! Thank you!"

The phone rang. It was her brother. "I've wanted a train set for years! And Jimmy loves his microscope," he said.

At the door, stern Aunt Susan beamed out from her hat and scarf.

"I was so fed up with *sensible* presents," she said. "These are such *fun*!"

"Well," said Mrs. Muddle, "what can Susie's brother Tom have got?"

Before she had time to work it out, Tom arrived.

"I've made you some cookies from my cookbook," he smiled. "It's a great present!"

Mrs. Muddle ate one of Tom's cookies. "I knew advance planning was the answer!" she laughed.

473

The First Noel

The first Noel the angels did say
Was to certain poor shepherds
In fields as they lay;
In fields where they lay,
Keeping their sheep,
On a cold winter's night
That was so deep.

Noel, Noel, Noel, Noel,
Born is the King of Israel!

They lookèd up and saw a star,
Shining in the East,
Beyond them far;
And to the earth it gave great light,
And so it continued both day and night.

474

And by the light of that same star,
Three wise men came
From country far;
To seek for a King was their intent,
And to follow the star
Wherever it went.

This star drew nigh
To the north-west;
O'er Bethlehem it took its rest,
And there it did both stop and stay
Right over the place where Jesus lay.

Noel, Noel, Noel, Noel,
Born is the King of Israel!

The Full House

"I don't know how we're going to manage this Christmas," said Mrs. Moore. "We're going to be full to the rafters."

"Yes, dear." Her husband was buried deep in his paper. He thought it best not to argue.

"Well, I had to invite your sister Maggie and her family when I heard that her new kitchen wouldn't be ready," explained Mrs. Moore.

"Yes, dear," said Mr. Moore. And he shuffled off to his tool shed.

476

The next day, Mr. Moore's time with the newspaper was interrupted again.

"I don't know where I'm going to put them all," he heard his wife say. "But I couldn't let Jimmy and his mother stay in that drafty old house over Christmas."

"You know best, dear. I'll be in the tool shed..." said Mr Moore.

On Christmas Eve, Mr. Moore had a surprise. His nightshirt was laid on a sleeping bag on the landing.

"Well, it's the only place for us to sleep," explained his wife.

"There is to be no more of this taking in of waifs and strays," replied Mr. Moore, "even at Christmas."

In fact, Mr. Moore enjoyed himself that evening, with so many people for supper. There were not enough chairs to go round but that didn't matter. Everyone was happy.

Just as they were all getting ready for bed, the doorbell rang. On the doorstep stood a young woman with a tiny baby.

"I heard that you help people," she said. "There was a fire in our street and everything is still drying out. We've nowhere to go tonight. We don't need much. The floor will be fine."

478

"I'm so sorry," said Mrs. Moore, "but I just have no room at all."

"Nonsense," said a voice behind her. It was Mr. Moore. "We'll just have to do a little reorganizing."

Later that night, Mr. Moore sighed contentedly. "This is really surprisingly comfortable," he said.

Mrs. Moore chuckled. "I know how fond *you* are of your tool shed," she said, "but I never expected this!"

479

Teddy Bear Christmas

On Christmas Eve, teddy bears find it just as hard to go to sleep as children do.

One Christmas Eve not long ago, Grandfather Bear tried everything to persuade the little ones to go to bed.

"If you don't go to sleep, a Very Important Visitor might not come *at all*," he warned. He tucked the little bears into bed and crept away.

Grandfather Bear snuggled into his own bed and turned off the light. But *could* he fall asleep? "I am a silly old bear," he said to himself, "to be excited about Christmas at *my* age."

480

And what were those noises at the door? Grandfather Bear smiled. "All right, you bad little teddy bears, I'll read you a story until you feel sleepy."

Grandfather Bear opened his special book of Teddy Bear stories. What do you think he read? "On Christmas Eve teddy bears find it just as hard to go to sleep as children do...."

We Wish You a Merry Christmas

We wish you a Merry Christmas,
We wish you a Merry Christmas,
We wish you a Merry Christmas
And a Happy New Year!

Glad tidings we bring
To you and your kin.
We wish you a Merry Christmas,
And a Happy New Year.

We wish you a Merry Christmas,
We wish you a Merry Christmas,
We wish you a Merry Christmas
And a Happy New Year!

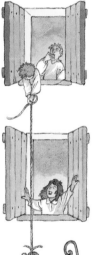

482

NURSERY RHYMES

Old Mother Goose,
When she wanted to wander,
Would ride through the air
On a very fine gander.

She had a son Jack,
A plain-looking lad,
He was not very good,
Nor yet very bad.

She sent him to market,
A live goose he bought:

"Here! Mother," says he,
"It will not go for naught."

Jack's goose and her gander
Grew very fond;
They'd both eat together,
Or swim in one pond.

Jack found one
    morning,
As I have been told,
His goose had laid
An egg of pure gold.

Jack rode to his mother,
The news for to tell.
She called him a good boy,
And said it was well.

Cackle, cackle,
    Mother Goose,
Have you any feathers
    loose?
Truly have I, pretty fellow,
Half enough to fill a pillow.
Here are quills,
Take one or two,
And down to make
A bed for you.

Little Boy Blue,
Come blow your horn,
The sheep's in the meadow,
The cow's in the corn.

Where is the boy
Who looks after the sheep?
He's under the haystack,
Fast asleep!

Will you wake him?
No, not I!
For if I do,
He's sure to cry.

486

Little Bo-Peep
    Has lost her sheep,
And doesn't know where to find them.
    Leave them alone,
    And they'll come home,
Bringing their tails behind them.

I had a little nut tree,
Nothing would it bear
But a silver nutmeg
And a golden pear.

The King of Spain's daughter
Came to visit me,
And all for the sake
Of my little nut tree.

All things bright and beautiful,
All creatures great and small,
All things wise and wonderful,
The Lord God made them all.

Jack and Jill went up the hill,
To fetch a pail of water;
Jack fell down and broke his crown,
And Jill came tumbling after.

Mary, Mary, quite contrary,
How does your garden grow?
With silver bells,
And cockle shells,
And pretty maids
   all in a row.

Curly Locks, Curly Locks, wilt thou be mine?
Thou shalt not wash dishes,
Nor yet feed the swine;
   But sit on a cushion and sew a fine seam,
   And feed upon strawberries,
                sugar and cream.

490

Hickory, dickory, dock,
The mouse ran up the clock.
The clock struck one,
The mouse ran down,
Hickory, dickory, dock.

Six little mice sat down to spin;
Pussy passed by, and she peeped in.
What are you doing, my little men?
Weaving coats for gentlemen.
Shall I come in and cut off your
    threads?
No, no, Mistress Pussy, you'd
    bite off our heads.

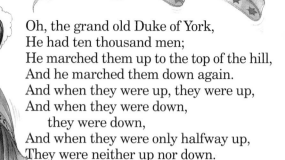

Oh, the grand old Duke of York,
He had ten thousand men;
He marched them up to the top of the hill,
And he marched them down again.
And when they were up, they were up,
And when they were down,
    they were down,
And when they were only halfway up,
They were neither up nor down.

For want of a nail, the shoe was lost,
For want of a shoe, the horse was lost,
For want of a horse, the rider was lost,
For want of a rider, the battle was lost,
For want of a battle, the kingdom was lost,
And all for the want of a horseshoe nail.

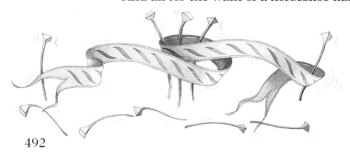

The lion and the unicorn
Were fighting for the
    crown;
The lion beat the unicorn
All around the town.

Some gave them white bread,
And some gave them brown;
Some gave them plum cake,
And drummed them out
    of town.

493

Solomon Grundy, born on Monday,
Christened on Tuesday,
    Married on Wednesday,
Took ill on Thursday,
    Worse on Friday,
Died on Saturday,
    Buried on Sunday,
That was the end
Of Solomon Grundy.

Old King Cole
Was a merry old soul,
And a merry old soul was he;
He called for his pipe,
And he called for his bowl,
And he called for his fiddlers three.
Every fiddler, he had a fine fiddle,
And a very fine fiddle had he;
Twee tweedle dee, tweedle dee, went
    the fiddlers.
Oh, there's none so rare as can compare
With King Cole and his fiddlers three.

Georgie Porgie,
Pudding and pie,
Kissed the girls
And made them cry.
When the boys
Came out to play,
Georgie Porgie
Ran away.

Doctor Foster
Went to Gloucester
In a shower of rain;
He stepped in a puddle,
Right up to his middle,
And never went there again.

495

One, two, buckle my shoe;
Three, four, knock on the door;
Five, six, pick up sticks;
Seven, eight, lay them straight;
Nine, ten, my fat hen;
Eleven, twelve, dig and delve;
Thirteen, fourteen, maids a-courting;
Fifteen, sixteen, maids in the kitchen;
Seventeen, eighteen, maids in waiting;
Nineteen, twenty, my plate's empty.

Tinker, tailor, soldier, sailor,
Rich man, poor man, beggar man, thief.

Where are you going to,
    my pretty maid?
I'm going a-milking, sir, she said.
May I come with you, my pretty maid?
Yes, if you like, kind sir, she said.
What is your fortune, my pretty maid?
My face is my fortune, sir, she said.
Then I cannot marry you, my pretty maid.
Nobody asked you, sir, she said.

Oranges and lemons,
Say the bells of St. Clement's.

You owe me five farthings,
Say the bells of St. Martin's.

When will you pay me?
Say the bells of Old Bailey.

When I grow rich,
Say the bells of Shoreditch.

When will that be?
Say the bells of Stepney.

I'm sure I don't know,
Says the great bell of Bow.

London Bridge is falling down,
    Falling down, falling down,
London Bridge is falling down,
    My fair lady.

Build it up with wood and clay,
    Wood and clay, wood and clay,
Build it up with wood and clay,
    My fair lady.

Wood and clay will wash away,
    My fair lady.

Build it up with bricks and mortar,
    My fair lady.

Little Jack Horner
Sat in a corner,
Eating his Christmas pie.
He put in his thumb,
And pulled out a plum,
And said, "What a good
    boy am I!"

Jack Sprat could eat no fat,
His wife could eat no lean,
And so between them both, you see,
They licked the platter clean.

Yankee Doodle went to town,
Riding on a pony;
He stuck a feather in his cap
And called it macaroni.

Little Tommy Tucker
Sings for his supper;
What shall we give him?
Brown bread and butter.
How shall he cut it
Without a knife?
How will he be married
Without a wife?

Tom, Tom, the piper's son,
He learned to play when he was
        young,
And all the tune that he could play
Was "Over the hills and far away."
Over the hills and a great way off,
The wind shall blow my topknot off.

Tom, Tom, the piper's son,
Stole a pig and away did run;
The pig was eat
And Tom was beat,
And Tom went howling
        down the street.

The man in the moon
Came down too soon
And asked the way to Norwich;
He went by the south
And burned his mouth
By eating cold plum
porridge.

Hot cross buns!
Hot cross buns!
One a penny,
Two a penny,
Hot cross buns!
If you have no daughters,
Give them to your sons,
One a penny,
Two a penny,
Hot cross buns!

Pease porridge hot,
Pease porridge cold,
Pease porridge in the pot,
Nine days old.

503

Little Miss Muffet sat on a tuffet,
Eating her curds and whey.
Along came a spider,
Who sat down beside her,
And frightened Miss Muffet away.

Eensy, weensy spider,
Climbing up the spout,
Along came the rain
And washed the spider
    out!

There was a crooked man,
And he walked a crooked mile,
He found a crooked sixpence
Against a crooked stile;
He bought a crooked cat,
Which caught a crooked mouse,
And they all lived together
In a little crooked house.

It's raining, it's pouring,
The old man is snoring.
He went to bed
And bumped his head,
And couldn't get up
In the morning!

505

Sing a song of sixpence,
    A pocket full of rye;
Four and twenty blackbirds,
    Baked in a pie.
When the pie was opened,
    The birds began to sing;
Wasn't that a dainty dish
    To set before a King?
The King was in his counting house,
    Counting out his money;
The Queen was in the pantry
    Eating bread and honey.
The maid was in the garden,
    Hanging out the clothes,
When down came a blackbird,
    And pecked off her nose!

The Queen of Hearts
She made some tarts,
All on a summer's day;
The Knave of Hearts
He stole the tarts,
And took them right away.
The King of Hearts
Called for the tarts,
And beat the Knave full sore;
The Knave of Hearts
Brought back the tarts,
And vowed he'd steal no more.

Bobby Shafto's gone to sea,
Silver buckles on his knee;
He'll come back and marry me,
Bonny Bobby Shafto!

Bobby Shafto's bright and fair,
Combing down his yellow hair,
He's my love forever more,
Bonny Bobby Shafto!

I saw a ship a-sailing,
A-sailing on the sea,
And oh, but it was laden
With pretty things for thee!

There were comfits in the cabin
And apples in the hold;
The sails were made of silk
And the masts were all of gold!

The four and twenty sailors
Who stood between the decks
Were four and twenty white mice
With chains about their necks.

The captain was a duck
With a packet on his back,
And when the ship began
    to move,
The captain said,
    "Quack! Quack!"

See-saw, Margery Daw,
Jacky shall have a new master;
He shall have but a penny a day,
Because he can't work any faster!

Humpty Dumpty sat on a wall,
Humpty Dumpty had a great fall.
All the King's horses
And all the King's men
Couldn't put Humpty together again.

Here we go 'round the mulberry bush,
The mulberry bush,
The mulberry bush,
Here we go 'round the mulberry bush,
On a cold and frosty morning.
This is the way we wash our clothes,
Wash our clothes,
Wash our clothes,
This is the way we wash our clothes,
On a cold and frosty morning.

Ring-a-ring-a-roses,
A pocket full of posies.
A-tishoo! A-tishoo!
We all fall down!

To market, to market, to buy a fat pig,
Home again, home again, jiggety jig.
To market, to market, to buy a fat hog,
Home again, home again, jiggety jog.

This little piggy went to market,
This little piggy stayed at home,
This little piggy had roast beef,
This little piggy had none.
And this little piggy cried,
"Wee, wee, wee," all the way home!

There was an old woman who lived in a shoe,
She had so many children,
She didn't know what to do.
She gave them some broth without any bread,
And scolded them soundly
And sent them to bed.

Girls and boys, come out to play,
The moon doth shine as bright as day.
Leave your supper and leave your sleep,
Come with your playfellows into the street.
Come with a whoop, and come with a call,
Come with a good will, or come not at all.

513

Old Mother Hubbard
Went to the cupboard
To fetch her poor dog
   a bone.
But when she got there,
The cupboard was bare,
And so the poor dog
   had none.

She sent to the baker's
To buy him some bread;
But when she came back,
The poor dog was dead.

She took a clean dish
To get him some tripe;
But when she came back,
He was smoking a pipe.

She went to the alehouse
To get him some beer;
But when she came back,
The dog sat in a chair.

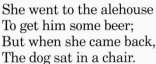

She went to the tailor's
To buy him a coat;
But when she came back,
He was riding a goat.

She went to the hatter's
To buy him a hat;
But when she came back,
He was feeding the cat.

She went to the cobbler's
To buy him some shoes;
But when she came back,
He was reading the news.

She went to the hosier's
To buy him some hose;
But when she came back,
He was dress'd in his
    clothes.

The dame made a curtsy,
The dog made a bow;
The dame said, "Your servant,"
The dog said, "Bow-wow."

Mary had a little lamb,
Its fleece was white as snow;
And everywhere that Mary went,
The lamb was sure to go.

It followed her to school one day,
That was against the rule;
It made the children laugh and play
To see a lamb at school.

"Why does the lamb love Mary so?"
The eager children cry;
"Why, Mary loves the lamb, you know,"
The teacher did reply.

Baa, baa, black sheep,
Have you any wool?
Yes, sir, yes, sir,
Three bags full.
One for my master,
And one for my dame,
And one for the little boy
Who lives down the lane.

The north wind doth blow,
And we shall have snow,
And what will poor robin do then,
Poor thing?
He'll sit in a barn,
And keep himself warm,
And hide his head under his wing,
Poor thing.

A wise old owl
Lived in an oak;
The more he saw,
The less he spoke;
The less he spoke,
The more he heard.
Why can't we all be
Like that wise old bird?

Polly, put the kettle on,
Polly, put the kettle on,
Polly, put the kettle on,
We'll all have tea.

Sukey, take it off again,
Sukey, take it off again,
Sukey, take it off again,
They've all gone away.

Pat-a-cake, pat-a-cake, baker's man,
Bake me a cake as fast as you can;
Pat it and prick it and mark it with B,
And put it in the oven for baby and me.

Simple Simon met a pieman
Going to the fair;
Said Simple Simon to the pieman,
"Let me taste your wares."

Said the pieman to Simple Simon,
"Show me first your penny."
Said Simple Simon to the pieman,
"Indeed, I haven't any."

Simple Simon went a-fishing,
For to catch a whale;
All the water he had got
Was in his mother's pail.

519

Oh, dear, what can the matter be?
Dear, dear, what can the matter be?
Oh, dear, what can the matter be?
Johnny's so long at the fair.

He promised to buy me
A bunch of blue ribbons,
He promised to buy me
A bunch of blue ribbons,
He promised to buy me
A bunch of blue ribbons,
To tie up my bonny brown hair.

As I was going to St. Ives,
I met a man with seven wives.
Each wife had seven sacks,
Each sack had seven cats,
Each cat had seven kits.
Kits, cats, sacks and wives,
How many were going to St. Ives?

Half a pound of tuppenny rice,
Half a pound of treacle,
Mix it up and make it nice,
Pop goes the weasel!

521

Ride a cock-horse to Banbury Cross
To see a fine lady upon a white horse.
With rings on her fingers and bells
   on her toes,
She shall have music wherever she goes!

I had a little pony,
His name was Dapple Gray;
I lent him to a lady,
To ride a mile away.
She whipped him,
She slashed him,
She rode him through the mire;
I would not lend my pony now,
For all the lady's hire.

How many miles to Babylon?
Three score miles and ten.
Can I get there by candlelight?
Yes, and back again.
If your heels are nimble
    and light,
You may get there by
    candlelight.

Jack, be nimble,
Jack, be quick,
Jack, jump over the candlestick!

Higgledy, piggledy,
My black hen,
She lays eggs
For gentlemen.

Goosey, goosey, gander,
Whither shall I wander?
Upstairs, downstairs,
And in my lady's chamber.
There I met an old man,
Who wouldn't say his prayers.
I took him by the left leg
And threw him down the
stairs.

524

Cock-a-doodle-doo!
My dame has lost her shoe!
My master's lost his fiddling stick
And doesn't know what to do!

Cock-a-doodle-doo!
What is my dame to do?
'Till master finds his fiddling stick,
She'll dance without her shoe!

Cock-a-doodle-doo!
My dame has found her shoe.
And master's found his fiddling stick,
Sing doodle-doodle-doo!

I love little pussy,
Her coat is so warm,
And if I don't hurt her
She'll do me no harm.
So I'll not pull her tail,
Nor drive her away,
But pussy and I
Very gently will play.

Hey diddle, diddle,
The cat and the fiddle,
The cow jumped over
    the moon.
The little dog laughed
To see such sport,
And the dish ran away
    with the spoon.

Ding, dong, bell,
Pussy's in the well.
Who put her in?
Little Johnny Green.
Who pulled her out?
Little Tommy Stout.
What a naughty boy was that
To try to drown poor pussycat.

Pussycat, pussycat,
Where have you been?
I've been up to London
To look at the Queen.
Pussycat, pussycat,
What did you there?
I frightened a little mouse
Under her chair.

Little Tommy Tittlemouse
Lived in a little house;
He caught fishes
In other men's ditches.

Little Polly Flinders
Sat among the cinders,
Warming her pretty little toes;
Her mother came and caught her,
And whipped her little daughter
For spoiling her nice new clothes.

Tweedledum and Tweedledee
Agreed to fight a battle,
For Tweedledum said Tweedledee
Had spoiled his nice new rattle.
Just then flew by a monstrous crow,
As black as a tar barrel,
Which frightened both the heroes so,
They quite forgot their battle.

Peter, Peter, pumpkin eater,
Had a wife and couldn't keep her;
He put her in a pumpkin shell,
And there he kept her very well.

Lavender's blue, dilly, dilly,
Lavender's green;
When I am King, dilly, dilly,
You shall be Queen.

Call up your men, dilly, dilly,
Set them to work,
Some to the plough, dilly, dilly,
Some to the cart.

Some to make hay, dilly, dilly,
Some to thresh corn,
While you and I, dilly, dilly,
Keep ourselves warm.

Rub-a-dub-dub,
Three men in a tub,
And how do you think they got there?
The butcher, the baker,
The candlestick-maker,
They all jumped out
Of a rotten potato,
'Twas enough to make
a man stare!

Three wise men of Gotham,
They went to sea in a bowl,
And if the bowl had been stronger,
My song had been longer.

Dance to your Daddy,
    My little laddie,
Dance to your Daddy,
    My little lamb!
You shall have a fishy
    On a little dishy,
You shall have a fishy
    When the boat comes in.

532

Pretty maid, pretty maid,
Where have you been?
Gathering roses
To give to the Queen.
Pretty maid, pretty maid,
What gave she you?
She gave me a diamond
As big as my shoe.

Monday's child is fair of face,
Tuesday's child is full of grace,
Wednesday's child is full of woe,
Thursday's child has far to go,
Friday's child is loving and giving,,
Saturday's child works hard for a living,
But the child that is born on the
    Sabbath day
Is bonny and blithe, and good, and gay.

I do not like thee, Doctor Fell,
The reason why I cannot tell;
But this I know, I know right well,
I do not like thee Doctor Fell.

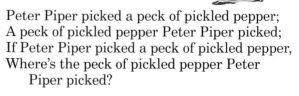

My mother said, I never should
Play with the gypsies in the wood.
If I did, she would say,
"Naughty little girl to disobey!"

Peter Piper picked a peck of pickled pepper;
A peck of pickled pepper Peter Piper picked;
If Peter Piper picked a peck of pickled pepper,
Where's the peck of pickled pepper Peter
    Piper picked?

Blow, wind, blow! And go, mill, go!
    That the miller may grind his corn;
    That the baker may take it,
    And into bread make it,
And bring us a loaf in the morn.

Two little birds sat
On a wall,
One named Peter,
One named Paul.
Fly away, Peter!
Fly away, Paul!
Come back, Peter!
Come back, Paul!

535

Three blind mice,
See how they run!
They all ran after the farmer's wife,
Who cut off their tails with a carving knife,
Did ever you see such a sight in your life,
As three blind mice?

A cat came fiddling out of a barn,
With a pair of bagpipes under her arm;
She could sing nothing but "Fiddle-de-dee,
The mouse has married the bumble bee."
Pipe, cat; dance, mouse;
We'll have a wedding at our good house.

Three little kittens
They lost their mittens
And they began to cry,
Oh mother dear, we sadly fear
That we have lost our mittens.
What! Lost your mittens,
You naughty kittens?
Then you shall have no pie.
Mee-ow, mee-ow, mee-ow,
No, you shall have no pie.

The three little kittens
They found their mittens
And they began to cry,
Oh mother dear, see here, see here,
For we have found our mittens.
Put on your mittens,
You silly kittens,
And you shall have some pie.
Purr-r, purr-r, purr-r,
Oh, let us have some pie.

I see the moon,
And the moon sees me.
God bless the moon,
And God bless me.

Wee Willie Winkie
Runs through the town,
Upstairs and downstairs,
In his nightgown.
Rapping at the window,
Crying through the lock,
"Are all the children in their beds,
It's past eight o'clock?"

POEMS
FOR
CHILDREN

I Started Early

I started Early—Took my Dog—
And visited the Sea—
The Mermaids in the Basement
Came out to look at me—

And Frigates—in the Upper Floor
Extended Hempen Hands—
Presuming Me to be a Mouse—
Aground—upon the Sands—

But no Man moved Me—till the Tide
Went past my simple Shoe—
And past my Apron—and my Belt
And past my Bodice—too—

And made as He would eat me up—
As wholly as a Dew
Upon a Dandelion's Sleeve—
And then—I started—too—

And He—He followed—close behind—
I felt His Silver Heel
Upon my Ankle—Then my Shoes
Would overflow with Pearl—

Until We met the Solid Town—
No One He seemed to know—
And bowing—with a Mighty look—
At me—The Sea withdrew—

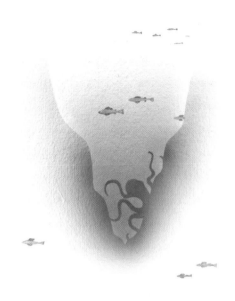

What Are Heavy?

What are heavy? sea-sand and sorrow:
What are brief? today and tomorrow:
What are frail? Spring blossoms and youth:
What are deep? the ocean and truth.

Full Fathom Five

Full fathom five they father lies;
Of his bones are coral made;
Those are pearls that were his eyes:
Nothing of him that doth fade,
But doth suffer a sea-change
Into something rich and strange:
Sea nymphs hourly ring his knell.
Ding-dong!
Hark! now I hear them,
Ding-dong, bell!

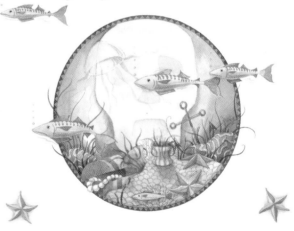

Foreign Lands

Up into the cherry-tree
Who should climb but little me?
I held the trunk with both my hands
And looked abroad on foreign lands.

I saw the next-door garden lie,
Adorned with flowers before my eye,
And many pleasant places more
That I had never seen before.

I saw the dimpling river pass
And be the sky's blue looking-glass;
The dusty roads go up and down
With people tramping in to town.

If I could find a higher tree
Farther and farther I should see,
To where the grown-up river slips
Into the sea among the ships,

To where the roads on either hand
Lead onward into fairy land,
Where all the children dine at five,
And all the playthings come alive.

Monday's Child

Monday's child is fair of face,
Tuesday's child is full of grace,
Wednesday's child is full of woe,
Thursday's child has far to go,
Friday's child is loving and giving,
Saturday's child works hard for his living,
And the child that is born on the Sabbath day
Is bonny and blithe, and good and gay.

A Child's Grace

Here a little child I stand
Heaving up my either hand;
Cold as paddocks though they be,
Here I lift them up to Thee,
For a benison to fall
On our meat and on us all.
Amen.

Is the Moon Tired?

Is the moon tired? She looks so pale
      Within her misty veil;
She scales the sky from east to west,
      And takes no rest.

Before the coming of the night
      The moon shows papery white;
Before the dawning of the day
      She fades away.

Star Light, Star Bright

Star light, star bright,
First star I see tonight,
I wish I may, I wish I might,
Have the wish I wish tonight.

How Many Miles to Babylon?

How many miles to Babylon?
Three score miles and ten.
Can I get there by candlelight?
Yes, and back again.
If your heels are nimble and light,
You may get there by candlelight.

Hush Little Baby

Hush little baby, don't say a word,
Papa's going to buy you a
    mockingbird.
If that mockingbird won't sing,
Papa's going to buy you a diamond ring.
If that diamond ring turns brass,
Papa's going to buy you a looking glass.
If that looking glass gets broke,
Papa's going to buy you a billy goat.
If that billy goat won't pull,
Papa's going to buy you a cart and bull.
If that cart and bull fall down,
You'll still be the sweetest little baby in town.

Winter

When icicles hang by the wall,
And Dick the shepherd blows his nail,
And Tom bears logs into the hall,
And milk comes frozen home in pail;
When blood is nipped, and ways be foul,
Then nightly sings the staring owl.
Tu-whit, tu-who! a merry note,
While greasy Joan doth keel the pot.

The Human Seasons

Four seasons fill the measure of the year;
There are four seasons in the mind of man:
He has his lusty Spring, when fancy clear
Takes in all beauty with an easy span:

He has his Summer, when luxuriously
Spring's honey'd cud of youthful thought he loves
To ruminate, and by such dreaming nigh
His nearest unto heaven: quiet coves

His soul has in its Autumn, when his wings
He furleth close; contented so to look
On mists in idleness – to let fair things
Pass by unheeded as a threshold brook:

He has his Winter too of pale misfeature,
Or else he would forgo his mortal nature.

The Tyger

Tyger! Tyger! burning bright
In the forests of the night,
What immortal hand or eye
Could frame thy fearful symmetry?

In what distant deeps or skies
Burnt the fire of thine eyes?
On what wings dare he aspire?
What the hand dare seize the fire?

And what shoulder, & what art,
Could twist the sinews of thy
    heart?
And when thy heart began to beat,
What dread hand? & what dread
    feet?

What the hammer? what the chain?
In what furnace was thy brain?
What the anvil? what dread grasp
Dare its deadly terrors clasp?

When the stars threw down their
    spears,
And water'd heaven with their tears,
Did he smile his work to see?
Did he who made the Lamb make
    thee?

Tyger! Tyger! burning bright
In the forests of the night,
What immortal hand or eye,
Could frame thy fearful symmetry?

She Walks in Beauty

She walks in beauty, like the night
Of cloudless climes and starry skies;
And all that's best of dark and bright
Meet in her aspect and her eyes:
Thus mellowed to that tender light
Which heaven to gaudy day denies.

One shade the more, one ray the less,
Had half impaired the nameless grace
Which waves in every raven tress,
Or softly lightens o'er her face;
Where thoughts serenely sweet express
How pure, how dear their dwelling-place.

And on that cheek, and o'er that brow,
So soft, so calm, yet eloquent,
The smiles that win, the tints that glow,
But tell of days in goodness spent,
A mind at peace with all below,
A heart whose love is innocent.

La Belle Dame Sans Merci

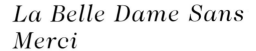

O what can ail thee, knight-at-arms,
Alone and palely loitering?
The sedge has wither'd from the lake,
And no birds sing.

O what can ail thee, knight-at-arms,
So haggard and so woe-begone?
The squirrel's granary is full,
And the harvest's done.

I see a lily on thy brow,
With anguish moist and fever dew;
And on thy cheeks a fading rose
Fast withereth too.

I met a lady in the meads,
Full beautiful – a faery's child,
Her hair was long, her foot was light,
And her eyes were wild.

I made a garland for her head,
And bracelets too, and fragrant zone;
She look'd at me as she did love,
And made sweet moan.

I set her on my pacing steed,
And nothing else saw all day long;
For sidelong would she bend, and sing
A faery's song.

She found me roots of relish sweet,
And honey wild, and manna dew,
And sure in language strange she said –
"I love thee true".

She took me to her elfin grot,
And there she wept and sigh'd full sore,
And there I shut her wild wild eyes
With kisses four.

And there she lulled me asleep
And there I dream'd – Ah! woe betide!
The latest dream I ever dream'd
On the cold hill side.

I saw pale kings and princes too,
Pale warriors, death-pale were they all;
They cried – "La Belle Dame sans Merci
Hath thee in thrall!"

I saw their starved lips in the gloam,
With horrid warning gaped wide,
And I awoke and found me here,
On the cold hill's side.

And this is why I sojourn here
Alone and palely loitering,
Though the sedge has wither'd from the lake,
And no birds sing.

A Child's Thought

At seven, when I go to bed,
I find such pictures in my head:
Castles with dragons prowling round,
Gardens where magic fruits are found;
Fair ladies prisoned in a tower,
Or lost in an enchanted bower;
While gallant horsemen ride by streams
That border all this land of dreams
I find, so clearly in my head
At seven, when I go to bed.

The Year's at the Spring

The year's at the spring
And day's at the morn;
Morning's at seven;
The hill-side's dew-pearled;
The lark's on the wing;
The snail's on the thorn:
God's in his heaven –
All's right with the world!

All Things Bright and Beautiful

All things bright and beautiful:
All creatures great and small,
All things wise and wonderful—
The Lord God made them all.

It's Raining, It's Pouring

It's raining, it's pouring,
The old man is snoring;
He went to bed and bumped his head
And couldn't get up in the morning!

Whether the Weather

Whether the weather be
    fine
Or whether the weather
    be not,
Whether the weather be
    cold
Or whether the weather
    be hot,
We'll weather the weather
Whatever the weather,
Whether we like it or not.

Hurt No Living Thing

Hurt no living thing;
Ladybird, nor butterfly,
Nor moth with dusty wing,
Nor cricket chirping cheerily,
Nor grasshopper so light of leap,
Nor dancing gnat, nor beetle fat,
Nor harmless worms that creep.

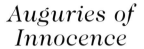

Auguries of Innocence

To see a World in a Grain of Sand
And a Heaven in a Wild Flower,
Hold Infinity in the palm of your hand
And Eternity in an hour.

A Robin Red breast in a Cage
Puts all Heaven in a Rage.
A dove house fill'd with doves &
    Pigeons
Shudders Hell thro' all its regions.
A dog starv'd at his Master's Gate
Predicts the ruin of the State.
A Horse misus'd upon the Road
Calls to Heaven for Human blood.
Each outcry of the hunted Hare
A fibre from the Brain does tear.
A Skylark wounded in the wing,
A Cherubim does cease to sing.
The Game Cock clip'd & arm'd for fight
Does the Rising Sun affright.
Every Wolf's & Lion's howl
Raises from Hell a Human Soul.

The wild deer, wand'ring here &
    there,
Keeps the Human Soul from Care.
The Lamb misus'd breeds Public
    strife
And yet forgives the Butcher's Knife.
The Bat that flits at close of Eve
Has left the Brain that won't Believe.
The Owl that calls upon the Night
Speaks the Unbeliever's fright.
He who shall hurt the little Wren
Shall never be belov'd by Men.
He who the Ox to wrath has mov'd
Shall never be by Woman lov'd.
The wanton Boy that kills the Fly
Shall feel the Spider's enmity.
He who torments the Chafer's sprite
Weaves a Bower in endless Night.
The Catterpiller on the Leaf
Repeats to thee thy Mother's grief.
Kill not the Moth nor Butterfly,
For the Last Judgment draweth nigh.

The Herring Loves the Merry Moonlight

The herring loves the merry moonlight,
The mackerel loves the wind,
But the oyster loves the dredging sang,
For they come of a gentle kind.

The Silver Swan

The silver swan, who living had no note,
When death approached, unlocked her silent
   throat,
Leaning her breast against the reedy shore,
Thus sung her first and last, and sung no more:
Farewell all joys! O death, come close mine eyes;
More geese than swans now live, more fools
   than wise.

The Wind

Who has seen the wind?
Neither I nor you;
But when the leaves hang trembling
The wind is passing through.

Who has seen the wind?
Neither you nor I;
But when the trees bow down their heads
The wind is passing by.

My Shadow

I have a little shadow that goes in and out
  with me,
And what can be the use of him is more than I
  can see.
He is very, very like me from the heels up to
  the head;
And I see him jump before me, when I jump
  into my bed.

The funniest thing about him is the way he
  likes to grow—
Not at all like proper children, which is always
  very slow;
For he sometimes shoots up taller like an
  india-rubber ball,
And he sometimes gets so little that there's
  none of him at all.

He hasn't got a notion of how children ought
    to play,
And can only make a fool of me in every sort
    of way.
He stays so close behind me he's a coward you
    can see;
I'd think shame to stick to nursie as that
    shadow sticks to me!

One morning, very early, before the sun
    was up,
I rose and found the shining dew on every
    buttercup;
But my lazy little shadow, like an arrant
    sleepy-head,
Had stayed at home behind me and was fast
    asleep in bed.

Index of Poets